Nefarious

by:

"No Sweat"

ITOH PRESS

ITOH PRESS
Bowling Green, KY 42103
www.itohpress.com

Nefarious by E. Lowell Robbins, Jr.
Cover Art by: Chesteen Robbins
Graphic Design by : Dalton Rowe
Editor: Abbey Piersma

Illustrations by:
Wallace Scott "Doc" Lewis, Irvine, Kentucky
Matthew Fish, Berea, Kentucky
Clark O'Dell, Boone Village, Kentucky
No Sweat, Richmond, Kentucky.

Public domain images provided by reusableart.com.

Print ISBN: 978-1-93-938307-5
Digital ISBN: 978-1-93-938307-5

Dedication:

Chesteen, Nancy, Lance, Barrett, Matt, "Lindy" Yeager, Guy
Davenport, Dave Cox, Eddie Woolery, Ed Hawkins and my darling
editor, Carol Itoh.

Acknowledgments:

My next door neighbor for seventeen years was "Lindy" Yeager, a
graduate of West Point and a captain in the Strategic Air Command
until his wife committed suicide. I learned much from him in the
way of music and literature. His door was always open with tea
and milk waiting. He inspired me to write the best I possibly could,
especially about those things people held within themselves. Before
he committed suicide he guided me to Guy Davenport, Rhodes
Scholar and recipient of the John D. MacArthur Genius Award.
Guy supposed me much older than I was when we first met at his
doorstep in Lexington, Kentucky. He had based my age on my novel,
THESE PRECIOUS DAYS. Lindy had sent him that manuscript
which Guy loved, stating that I was a real writer, the kind that would
have to own the hide of a rhino to find success. Writing was nothing
short of a religion for him. Guy always made time for me, giving
encouragement and scoffing at anyone that failed to recognize my
work, upsetting him as if it were his own.

Dear No Sweat,

NEFARIOUS is a terrible title for a book. Nobody would ever buy a book with that name. It is a word
that nobody understands. Since you will not entertain my editorial suggestion to change the title the Jesse Stuart Foundation will no longer consider publishing your book.

Jack Gifford

CEO & Senior Editor

January 26, 2011

"You come in and out of this world alone but as long as you are an outlaw you'll always have company."

~Reverend Moses Hawkins

"Nothing so proved that life was an illusion as a grave."

~Edward Hawkins

"You slept through your trial just like a baby."

~Judge Quinn

"There are only three things in this old world, red whiskey, red skies and redheaded women."

~Piano Red

Chapter One

Under a Sycamore

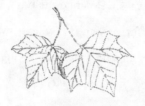

On one side of Moses was a black cat with big yellow eyes; he looked over at it, and then he looked up into the sky. What he saw made him pray.

"Oh Eater of Dreams be gone. Be gone from me. Be gone from my family. Be gone from all that I love. Be gone forever. Look not down on me. Dwell not in me. Allow me to dream. Allow my dream. Oh Eater of Dreams be gone. Amen."

Since dawn the Hawkins boys had been fishing quiet. The way the fog had disappeared off the water had been mystical leaving so many still souls wrapped on a tree's roots that they seemed almost a part of the roots themselves.

And maybe they were?

And the way the light filtered down upon their heads dappling in so many varying shades coming through such jagged and large leaves reflected yet something timeless and holy.

Now, an old buzzard, oddly enough, had lit out before the rest of his own family, showing up along the river. It swayed queer above the trees smelling, eyeballing, soaring and swooping and sometimes disappearing.

1

But it always came back. Below that buzzard sat all seventeen of the Hawkins boys; each was bad worried their mom was fixing to die. That buzzard was the last thing they needed to see... That Eater of Dreams.   The river always welcomed the boys. No matter the season she was there in her different way. But when it was summertime, like it was now, she called special with that same loving whisper as did their mom, kissing and asking them to awake.

Chapter Two

Molly's Order

When Moses showed up at his brother's cabin and then received
Molly's unexpected order to go fishing he paused before throwing
on a valiant smile. He thought her asking him to do such a thing was
ridiculous. But there was a lot going on nobody knew about; top secret
stuff only he and Molly know-d on.

Yesterday, when he had been sitting naked in a brass tub drinking
whiskey next to a stained glass window on the second floor of The
Eagle's Nest, Miss Chesteen's House of Venture, Kentucky's most
elegant house of ill repute, both of the naked gals that were with him,
Yevette, a green-eyed blonde from Scotland, and Sheniqua, a green-
eyed, black temptress from an island called, Eleuthera, complained, not
wanting him to leave. Sheniqua ranted that Eleuthera meant freedom.
And at that particular time that was what she wanted. But some things
were more important than a good time and he cut out, riding back
some sixty miles. "Molly," he said, once getting to the cabin, "I'll be
glad to do it. Fishing is good for a man. It restores the soul and builds
character."

Chapter Three

That Ol' Buzzard

"How long can something like that go before it ever flaps its wings?" asked Moses, looking back at the cat; its big eyes reminded him of a hoot owl's.

The old buzzard played the air, teeter-tottering with little effort, an end flight feather lifting ever so smart when needed. The Eater of Dreams eased to a height just above the sycamore. Was it the bird with fangs so anxious to erase our existence? A sparrow cocked his head and thought about flying up there and aggravating that terror, then held still letting things be.

Moses took a throwback; a stout warp of whiskey to his lips invariably causing his head to lean backwards. Over there on the bank on the other side of the river was a blue heron; it was holding still and also studying the water in its own sophisticated way.

Normally, he enjoyed being alone, resolving years ago that the best company was a campfire. But now he had never seen so many redheads. Between his brother and Molly, redheads would never go extinct.

"Red," he upped and thundered, "is God's color. And redheads are God's most dear children. After God busted up the darkness and made light the next thing he worked on was creating red. Red is everything in the Bible. Blood, fire, war, you name it. Every rainbow begins with that color. Did you know that it had to be a red heifer that was required for sacrifice for cleansing and purification? And poor Jesus, when them Romans was givin' him hell, they stripped him down and throw-d a red robe on him!"

Moses set his bottle back between his legs and took off his preacher's collar. No need to show off for this bunch, he thought. They're the best congregation, ever. They bad need that one story, something to get there downed heads off Molly.

Another throwback of whiskey went down.

Moses pondered a spell and then broke loose. "Once upon a time me and your daddy come a-floatin' down this very stretch," he declared. "It was back when we was mere nothing's…"

The boys perked up. To them, larks made foolish music compared to Moses' ragged confab. Fishing instantly took second place. No one compared to Moses. He stood alone. His stories had such a way of playing through their minds and hypnotizing the moment.

Moses paused, moving his head upstream, putting on a show of melancholy, gazing off to a spot somewhere in the middle of the river way up there along the far bend. "Perhaps it was all a nefarious dream," he sighed as his voice trailed off.

Each boy was slumped but alert. Of all Moses' stories, this one was by far their favorite. They could listen to it until they died.

Moses took another long pause, staring at the river. You could see him somehow attempting to hard remember on things. What a performance. "When we got to right out there," he confided, nodding upstream, "That's when we two nothing's met him -- the great catfish."

All the boys lifted their heads and stared upstream. Even though they owned reservations about the story they couldn't help but wonder.

Moses lit a cigar.

Straight down in front of him, a clear path led between two boys to the family's strongest pole. Canepole had chopped down that pole with an axe and named it Luke; it was the one pole reserved for that certain catfish; a pole thirteen feet long, bigger round than any strong man's arm, made out of ironwood and featuring a heavy iron collar at its end. Out past the pole, a leaf had floated along, hooking where the pole's line touched into the water; on the leaf, two metallic colored snake doctors were messing around, forming a shiny blue "M".

Smoke rings drifted about, expanding and disappearing as a Belted Kingfisher made its loud, dry rattling noise while undulating in flight down the river.

Moses held quiet.

"Down the river of doom all through the night," interposed Canepole, grabbing his turn to tell the family story, "floated us nothing's. Wide-eyed and bushy-tailed, we were, grinning like possums. We'd no more than left the watery confines of our momma's pooched belly than did we find ourselves in another slimy situation. On both sides of this river was Chief Blackfish's devil bunch -- which couldn't swim nary lick--watching our basket. Their arrows and spears hit and splashed all around but we never paid no mind. The world what we'd been sweet seeing had been nothing but magic; stars, bullfrogs and fish and sometimes a turtle jumping off a log. We didn't know nothing about no Injuns or what had happened to our poor mom and dad; nothing about no dying. All we know-d, we was floating easy and being rocked by the gentlest of all creatures, The Miss Green Enchantress herself, Mamma River."

Canepole paused, taking a rag out of his back pocket, wiping it across his eyes to help dispose of the incredible tears that he had somehow produced. As Moses' ears took in Canepole's river tale he was itching to tell his nephews about that time he once walked alongside a grouse for an hour, the time he slept in a cave with ten thousand grand daddy longlegs bunched up and roosting over his face and about the time he found that Indian jug half as big as him, full of green flint knives. Those stories needed telling, for sure, but not now.

The boys looked back one at a time to observe their father's performance, anxious for the oratory to continue. "What happened next?" asked Matthew, looking at his pet box terrapin he had mounted on his knee, its shell owned a patchwork of brown, yellow and black scales; and it had all four legs and its head poked out and was moving about trying to crawl but only able to flap its legs in the air as if it were flying or swimming in imaginary water.

"When the next morning came," confided Canepole, "the sunshine smacked in our basket, bounced off our faces and spread across the water. We looked at the shiny surface and we saw a buzzard circling above us. We couldn't make out what it was. Y'see, babies eyes are poor and all. I don't know why, but that bird struck us as funny. We took to laughing something awful, playing peep-eye with the thing. We loved the game so much we never thought about getting hungry or messing in our drawers. We laid there until suddenly a whirlpool took a-hold on us."

"The catfish?" asked Matthew, interrupting.

"Yep." responded Canepole. "Y'see, the catfish can pick up on the slightest noise. When it detected us, it come a-sneaking out of its deep hole commencing to employ its own tactics, something the way a pup does when it chases its tail, only worser. The great fish knows all about drowning; has it down to an art. When it gets to going fast enough, it can cause an underwater tornado what'll suck down anything on the surface. Sink it straight to the bottom. And after whatever it is has drowned and gone rotten then comes the catfish easing along with a smile on its face, a-licking its chops."

"Boys," interrupted Moses, "When me and your daddy first come down this river we were all smiles on the insides of that poor basket. That's a fact. Then our world took to spinning. We got to going so fast our world warn't nothing but a blur--."

"It's been a blur ever since. And that's more a fact," interrupted Canepole, lifting the bottle, throwinback.

"That it has been brother, that it has been, amen," agreed Moses, re-claiming the bottle, continuing. "When at last we took to going so fast my instincts allowed we was in peril, I busted loose with a squall that stripped the leaves off every tree down river for over a mile. The whole town of Irvine heard me. They dropped everything they was doing and run straight out onto the old rope bridge that use to swang here; it run over there from that cliff and crossed over the river down to them fields. Anyways, DaddyJim, what always fished right here, quit fooling with his pole and done himself a headfirst. Everybody on the bridge watched as he angled off upstream packing a knife in his jaws. Nary a soul, except him, actually know-d what it was that was a-stirring under our basket and a-causing that whirlpool that we nothings was captured in. Nobody, except DaddyJim, know-d it were the true king of all catfish, the gen-u-wine, actual great, great, granddaddy of them all!" Moses paused once more, taking his eyes off the river. He looked up. That buzzard was still there. At times, the way the morning sun hit it, it appeared almost silvery. Something about those outstretched wings reminded him of Canepole. That way he would show out when he would make one his cliff dives. Looking over at his brother, Moses noticed that he was solemn, staring at the water down there below the surface at a brown leaf with mold on it. Moses knew that look. Hope was hanging frail.

Canepole felt Moses' eyes rubbing on him. "I'm thankful my prodigal brother is here," he acknowledged, "At the same time I'm rather ashamed, something as serious as Molly's chances. And yet, uncontrollably so, I keep thinking about the many reports on how big catfish have been hitting all week; Crawdads, night crawlers, minnows – they've been biting on anything. Every day in a river that appears as liquid jade, somebody has been catching a catfish bigger than the day before. It just ain't right the way my heart is messed up, is it? And I've also been sitting here and thinking about what all happened yesterday morning right after Molly had asked for you. That's when I gathered up all my boys around my horse. There's no telling where your Uncle Moses is right now, I told them. But with it fixing to be Saturday night and all, he'll likely be at The Eagle's Nest. I explained that it was a good sixty miles to get there, if you cut a straight trail. All them argued for who would get to go, one getting a black eye in the struggle. But it was Lowell that was chosen. I rubbed my hand over Lowell's head and explained my decision to the rest. Lowell's light, I told them. None of you can outswim or outfish him. He knows how to listen to a horse. Mainly though, he's lucky. If it were just a matter of desire, I'd ride myself. A minute later after Lowell mounted up I asked him to lean over while I looked him hard in the eye. Son, stay low and ride smart, I ordered. If Moses gets here in time, mom might live. If this horse dies, she dies."

Chapter Four

Still Circlin'

Now Moses looked away from the buzzard and took a magnanimous throwback. "Ashes to ashes, dust to dust, keep your gullet oiled and you'll never rust," he reded, after catching his breath. "A man's worth lays in his storytelling.

In the right hands a story is an axe in life's terrible wilderness," he preached as he looked back into the sky. "The difference in the way a man sees himself is in the stories he knows and the stories he tells."

Moses took back up where he had left off.

"You boys need to know that the town of Irvine had always looked down on DaddyJim. Y'see, Irvine didn't care much for DaddyJim because he warn't no bragger. Didn't own no property. Didn't do no work. Didn't let on about what he thought or what he was ever going to do. Not DaddyJim. The only thing DaddyJim ever had to say was something about fishing. People would holler, 'How they a-bitin' today, Jim!' And DaddyJim, he'd holler back, 'Lo-o-ord God! I've got me a hell-of-a-strang! Lookeehere!' And he would, too. He'd turn around and that string of them fish would start way up somewhere on his shoulder and run all the ways down his back and out anywhere from five to ten foot dragging behind him. There wasn't a day what the old man didn't bring in a string like that. 'Have ya seen that catfish?' they'd holler. And that would set him to going. 'I ain't see-d him today. If I had, I wouldn't be sittin' hyur!' he'd say.

Everybody would always laugh, wondering was Jim downing red whiskey or clear--But on the day DaddyJim dove in and swum upstream to save us nothing's nobody mentioned nothin' about no drankin'. Everybody was leaned out over that bridge and watching as DaddyJim doved under for five minutes before he come back up without his knife. All by his lonesome, he ended that whirlpool -- leastways, for the time being. Me and Canepole got saved only because DaddyJim caught that catfish off-guard. That catfish never dreamed nothing would ever come at him. That golden devil had been scouring around since Bible times. Wound up where it were -- deep out there -- because it got stuck during the drying out period that followed up after Noah's bunch.

DaddyJim never allowed that demon no chances: A sneak attack from the rear, he done. Cut bad straight into the monster's gizzard, bushwhacked the fish's pride. And for that one glorious moment

14

with everyone in Irvine looking and never knowing what really happened, DaddyJim sent that critter back to the bottom where it took and moseyed on up inside its old cave to lick its shameful wound. Licked and even cried a little. Causing a certain salty ripple that only DaddyJim know-d what was.

When DaddyJim come to the surface, he took a-hold of our basket and swum it back down the middle of the river and got out right here. Everybody was watching when he found the note tied to my neck. They studied on him when he took it off and commenced to reading on it. Of course, DaddyJim couldn't read a lick. 'What's the note say?' hollered down the people. DaddyJim didn't know what to say. He wanted us two baby boys more than anything. He kept looking up at all the people and then back down at us. He knew we didn't belong to nobody in Irvine because everybody in Irvine knows everything on everybody just the way it still does. He knew we'd survived coming down from Shawnee country. That chief Blackfish had took back on the warpath and was killing anything what so-much-as-took-a-breath.

DaddyJim knew the note was written in blood. That was plain to see. The signs told him who we was and what we was. 'They're little lost babies!' he hollered up to the bridge. 'Their ma and pa got tharselves butchered off by Injuns upstream!' Everybody on the bridge shook their heads. 'What-cha gonner do with 'em?' they hollered. 'Well,' he said, 'I'd sure like to keep 'em. Time has sure gone by slow, you'll never know. I've been waiting all these years to touch my two babies again. God has seen fit to send 'em back. Let me have 'em, Irvine! Please! For God'ssake let me have 'em! I'm -a-beggin'!

If everyrbody will say it's alright, I'd like to be their daddy and raise 'em up!'"

"Yessir," interrupted Canepole, "There was indeed a rare woman. One of the few in Irvine whatever owned a memory or a heart. She know-d DaddyJim's story. Know-d long before the citizens come along that DaddyJim had cleared the way. Know-d too, the thing what kept DaddyJim always at this spot.

Irvine looked down at DaddyJim. He was a loner. Nobody really knew nothing about him except that he always laid drunk on the river, fishing. Leaving two stranded babies with such a figure had them all perplexed, except for that one woman. She worked her way, climbing over and through that bunch on the bridge to where the bridge was sagging in the middle; she know-d the real history on Irvine and the story on ol' Jim. Know-d it was Jim that was the first white man ever to set foot in Estill County. How he had once put on a fierce fight against the Shawnee at this very spot. And if-n it weren't for Jim, there wouldn't've never been no Estill County."

Canepole stopped talking. He knew this day would be a two prong fishhook of fate; life dangling on one point, death smiling on the other. Things rarely went good in the hills. Somehow, the iron that was in the Kentucky dirt rubbed off on people's spirits. "You see, boys, Ol' Jim's babies had been the same age when they'd been sucked down by the catfish. He had tried to hold off them Shawnee led by Chief Blackfish but he knew them Injuns had him. He weren't no fool. He knew death comes for us all. It's the way a man prepares and faces it that shows what he is. He could see how them Shawnee was hid

16

behind every tree; a hundred or more. He set his wife and two young-
n's to hit the river and make a swim-for-it; them arrows and spears was
awful. But DaddyJim's wife was slick, holding a cradleboard over her
and her two baby boys as she made it out to the middle.

Then, the most awfullest thing happened; something that made
the Injuns stop and watch. A whirlpool took a-hold on DaddyJim's
wife and babies, taking them under. DaddyJim didn't know what
had happened, but the Injuns did. They knew the great catfish of all
catfish lived deep in that stretch. That panther, bear and elk had all
been sucked down by that fish at one time or another. They knew
that whenever the catfish got itself something that the river got safe
for a full moon. DaddyJim allowed, when chief Blackfish saw what
happened, he told his braves to scat, leaving DaddyJim all alone that
evening. And he'd stayed alone all them many long years until us
nothing's come floating along.

All them people on the bridge was just fixing to tell DaddyJim
to bring us two babies up to them. They were going to take us away
and see to it we wound up in proper hands, probably somewhere
over in Lexington. Nobody know-d how much DaddyJim's heart was
pounding except that one woman. Leslie Jones was her name. It was
her that knew not only the history of Estill County but also the truth.
She knew when Jim had fought his way into this country he lost his
wife and his own two baby boys to the catfish. 'Jim,' hollered that
woman. 'I represent Irvine! They've elected me their voice!'

17

Everybody on the bridge wondered if Leslie had been hitting the bottle again. They hadn't elected nobody nothing. Still, out of curiosity, they let her keep on hollering stuff without interrupting. 'Jim,' she said,' we've decided unanimously that you're the man to have them babies! I think Irvine has forgotten what happened to your wife and two young-n's. We want you to know, if-n the Lord can giveth and taketh away, well, by God, he can giveth again! You keep them boys, Jim, they're yours! You raise them up any way your heart sees fit! All we ask is that you love them forever--Without love none of us are nothin'!'

Nobody in Irvine spoke.

Leslie had said it all.

DaddyJim looked back up with big tears. 'I'm gonner raise 'em right, I swear!' he hollered to the crowd. 'I'm gonner give 'em all the love one man can! I'm gonner larn 'em on Jesus and all that stuff! But before I ever get around doing all that, I'm gonner teach 'em both to fish. Serious fish! Because there ain't nary a one of you realizes the danger out in this river! And you won't, nosir! Not until that fish gets caught! One of my boys or one of my grandchilds is going to catch that fish! Then, Irvine, you'll be safe at last!'

Chapter Five

Do Buzzards Die?

The boys loved listening to the Catfish story and going
back in time.

One of them, Matthew, looked up at a dead limb as Canepole told
the tale. Three small balls hung down from the sycamore branch,
each soft and ready to burst loose. Mixed there under so many narrow
shadows of the baby willows, the bank owned drifts of fine sand; tan
in color with bits of coal, dried clay and countless sparkles; fireflies
of the day. The river messed with Matthew's soul, easing his worries
and dreams downstream. His shirt was off as his freckles begged to
multiply. The brother closest to him, John, held an orange and black
dotted salamander. In a queer world of question this story gave each
boy a sense of home, putting their feet in the mud that made them.

Bear, the most emotional and stockiest of all the boys, always ready
to cry or laugh or kiss or fight in a second; a beautiful child with even
features and a brown mixture in his reddish hair that perfectly matched
his dark greenish-brown eyes, thought of the last time when all of
them had gathered like this but on a happier note. He remembered
what Moses had told him about the way life is: That sticks were

19

crooked, that the river was crooked and that spider webs were crooked. Nothing is fair in this world, he said. But you get a little time to live. Don't' waste it. Follow your dreams.

James, the oldest and tallest of the Hawkins boys, wiry and owning thick hair darker red than any of them, noticed a feather turned upside down floating by just beneath the surface. "Dad," he spoke, "Do buzzards die?"

Canepole's eyes hunkered down at James' turned face. "I'd like to believe they die," he answered with a morose heart. "But they don't. Every man has his own buzzard, always there."

"Buzzards die," interposed Moses, attempting to overshadow his brother but unable to escape the same laden heart. "I found one's skeleton," he declared, "Peered to be young; had a big mouth, likely died from curiosity."

One of the boys, Zeke, had a stick and was aiming it at the buzzard as it passed over, shooting at it in his mind. "Uncle Moses," he spoke. "You told us the last time you told the catfish story that you wished it was always summer and that the river was a current of green tears. Green tears, from what?"

"Angels," answered Moses. "When angels take a look down here and see how sweet our summer is it sets them to weeping jealous tears; Done nights, so you don't see them."

"Uncle Moses?"

"Yes?"

"Have you ever told a lie?"

20

The light through the sycamore canopy threw a strange life on Moses' cigar smoke; it was a light blue and swirled around as if some changing thought floating up to heaven. "Nephew," answered Moses. "Sacrificing the truth on occasion ain't nothing bad, preachers make an art of it, people know that. But they lie it ain't so. This world is full of lies. Daytime lets you think you're something special then night comes along. You look up and see the stars. The more you look at them the more you realize daytime lied. What's a poor lie when you live your life in a dream?"

One boy, Simon, looked at a blackbird facing toward the river; the bird owned a brilliant red patch on its shoulder and there was a yellow stripe just beneath the red; it kept flicking its tail up and down, fussing at everyone, somewhere its nest was near and this place was supposed to be his. "Ain't Chief Blackfish the one that chased Daniel Boone two hundred miles barefoot back to Fort Boonesborough?"

"Yep, same bird."

"Reckon where Blackfish got that name?"

"Don't know. But Blackfish sure messed up naming Daniel, calling him, Sheltowee, which means, Big Turtle. That day Daniel got loose from his bunch he didn't turn out to be no turtle."

"Did Jonah really get swallowed by a whale?" pushed Caleb, standing up to stretch, pulling out on his one suspender, looking towards Moses and that slick, black cat sitting content beside him; that cat wouldn't have much to do with anyone but when Moses came around he and it were inseparable. Of all the Hawkins tribe Caleb had the brightest red-orange hair; even a little yellow was in it.

Nobody could touch him on the amount of freckles he'd been blessed with. And for every freckle he seemed to have a question.

"Jonah allowed to his wife that the reason he'd been gone for three days and nights was because a whale swallowed him. Your daddy told the same tale to your mom one time. Only, it was the catfish instead of the whale. Your mom might not be able to see but she could see right through that."

"NEE-FAIR-EE-US," upped a voice from the bunch. "Reckon how much you've made off that word?"

Moses flipped some ashes. "Not so much."

Getting up to stretch, he put both hands up into the sky and looked at his fingers. If a hawk could have had hands they would have been like his. Simple folk scared of dying flocked to give him money for telling some Bible tale; And if he used the word "nefarious" in his sermon it strangely mesmerized his congregation for additional donations. Just like death, the big word was frightening, somehow producing money out of pockets.

Sneaky out there, beyond his fingers was that Eater of Dreams, still circling.

Moses saw him, alright.

When he eased back down he sat closer to Canepole. Their bodies didn't touch as much as did their hearts. Canepole re-lit his cigar and released a series of smoke rings as he looked over his left shoulder back up somewhere through the woods.

Chapter Six

Mind Breeze

Moses remembered himself back at The Eagle's Nest.

But now he was fishing with his nephews.

He thought of Vicky, that raven-haired, Spanish wildcat that no man could tame and no woman resist; she was the one having laid a wicked kiss on him before leading him to Chie, a Japanese gal who was downstairs playing "Chopin's Nocturne" on the piano; that music smoothed the air and took the edge off life's perplexities.

Then there appeared Miss Chesteen, Molly's twin sister; a personified rose of an eternal nature; an Irvine girl what had gone bad, too ashamed to go home and too proud to admit sorrow; she had thick, long, dark red hair, green eyes and ten thousand freckles; It was impossible for her ever to be cold as long as she wore that blanket of freckles. She was the owner of the house, caretaker of the cash, and without argument, The Eagle's Nest's stellar attraction. "A WOMAN WITHOUT FRECKLES IS LIKE A NIGHT WITHOUT STARS," was her coy saying which was also inscribed over her bedroom door.

In the middle of her room, off along the back wall near the bed, there was an enormous stained glass window showing two red-headed mermaids playing in a river on a full moon with a cone-shaped, well known Estill county mountain named, Sweet Lick Knob, behind them; one of the mermaids was half out of the water and holding a Kentucky red agate in her hand and the other was showing off all of her nature in an innocent way until you saw her belly. From there on, she was all fish. In a way, proof that mankind had been around a long time.

Something about that stained glass window messed with Moses' mind. When Lowell's message about Molly got to him, he'd been soaking sweet, red-eyed fine with Yevette and Sheniqua, two of the choicest ladies to ever have blessed Kentucky. There was no other region in the entire world where they felt so free and yet, thanks to the politicians, expensive.

When Lowell and Vicky had come busting through his door at Miss Chesteen's, Yevette stood naked at one end of the tub, and Sheniqua, likewise bare, stood at the other end, counting aloud and waving a peacock tail-feather fan; they were counting out loud because Moses enjoyed showing off the Hawkins tradition on just how long he could stay submerged in a tub of water.

When he surfaced, he was surprised to see Vicky and Lowell standing right there before him.

"Uncle Moses," said Lowell, "Dad sent me. The family bad needs you. Momma's dying. We all thought mom was going to have her babies like she always does but things ain't gone right. She's calling for you. Says she needs you at her side. Uncle Moses, she's ten months pregnant. She ain't never gone that long. You've got to go. You have to. We're all counting on you. Please."

Never had a boy cried like Lowell. His heart and all of the Hawkins' hearts had burst loose in his swollen eyeballs.

That day, Moses rode tough, hunkered low on Miss Chesteen's horse, coattails flapping, an empty bottle every so often bursting somewhere. If he didn't make it he'd never forgive himself. No traveling preacher--even one that had to account to his congregation for his financial affairs--ever traveled so far so fast. Wild drunk, he raced, taking shortcuts that owned reputations with copperheads and rattlers, making blind jumps over ditches and creeks, homing in true. Twice, he and Miss Chesteen's red thoroughbred crossed stretches of the river.

Finally, he staggered through his brother's door noting the heavy smell of ashes. He passed by scattered bunk beds going three high and saw two different ladders leading up to the loft where more of the family slept. He came to the door of a room, Canepole's and Molly's familiar quarters. Two of the older girls were with them, sitting up on the floor with troubled expressions, their backs against the logs of the wall and their feet at the base of a double wide built cradle. In the cradle slept a set of twins. Next to the cradle, sitting beside Molly in bed, Canepole was sullen, worried sick, holding Molly's hand; she was weak and skinny, except for her belly; you could see the blue veins in her freckled hands. She looked upwards at him and smiled. She was blind, had been from birth, but knew he was there, recognizing his fast steps and the smell of his whiskey. He kneeled down beside her and took her hand. And then she and Canepole all three held each other. A fortune teller had once told Molly those freckles on her eyelids meant her family would have great fortune. Now, they wondered.

Never before had Moses seen his brother this scared, a soul battling so desperately against horror. It was almost as if he couldn't breathe. Canepole's long face was unshaven, his lips firm, his eyes swollen, hypnotized; disillusioned. How can I help? Moses thought. Being a man of the cloth he had seen death more than most, knew that it came in the morning more times than not. And knew its still embrace and the destruction it levied when a man watches his wife go. Then came those words out of Molly's mouth, "Fishin'. Go fishin'."

Moses couldn't believe Molly's orders.

"Her time is close," said Canepole. "She could go at any time."

Fishing was an awful idea but Moses couldn't think of nothing no better.

"Kiss her, Cane," he said. "Make it a kiss grateful for all the love she's give you. And then, brother, let's get the poles and go fishing. Let's take the boys and catch that catfish."

Chapter Seven

Butterflies in Heaven

Holding steady at the head of Catfish Creek Canepole
kept remembering him leaning over Molly, looking down into
her open eyes.

The whole family had squeezed in watching him as he raised her
body up as best he could into his arms giving her a hug, never wanting
to let go. Then he gave her a scared kiss before easing her back down,
giving her one last look; she was so pitiful and yet so brave.

Soon after, like so many soldierly phantoms going steadfast into
battle, the boys with shouldered poles disappeared for the river. A
half hour later, several of the boys set their prop stick "Y"s and then
reinforced the prop with another stick or rock. Once all the canes were
spread, silence fell. Some thought of Lowell:

Riding all the way over to Lexington and then straight back. If it
was one thing a Hawkins knew better than fishing, it was a horse.

Lowell had appeared like nothing had happened, taking up a position and remained silent, wetting a line.

As Lowell began fishing he took to dozing off remembering the past day.

It was one matter to find Moses, another to have ridden back like he'd done. In a still and silvery place on the water's surface, he, like Moses, kept remembering what experiences at The Eagle's Nest; Vicky's kiss, heavens. Vicky had opened the door, smiling, wearing a green silk robe, open down the middle. Behind her was Mint, a seventeen-year-old Injun gal with a white streak in her long hair, an albinism found among the Mandan females, a feature donated to them as a result of admixture with Prince Madoc's lost Welsh colonists. Mint was wearing an elk skin ornamented with elk's teeth and red agate beads. "I've got to get my Uncle Moses. Mom's dying," he insisted.

Vicky began to lead Lowell to another room when a divine creature happened to be easing down the stairs; she owned a face more honest than death and her curves -- they put the bends in the river to shame. Stark, she were, freckles only, nearly jaybird naked, except-n for her high boots with cathead spurs, a black panther's fur hide around her waist and a candelabra in her hand. Trailing alongside her were three bushy-tailed cats; Maine Coons, descendants from Mary Queen of Scots' six what had somehow snuck to America; black and gold lionesses with spell-throwing yellow eyes.

"Welcome to The Eagle's Nest," the redhead greeted, not recognizing that it was one of her nephews all grown up. "This is my home for the lost and misdirected. I'm Miss Chesteen, anything your heart desires, you let me know."

28

It must have been a dream, pondered Lowell, while he continued to fish.

Then, he glanced up and saw that bird that loved death causing his mind to circle back to where he was, to the place and time now there with his brothers on the river.

Mom is all we have, he realized. Without her, we're nothing.

Moses was trying to hold quiet, riled that life was such a bizarre mess. Who could dream such a mean dream that owned death? He wished he could fight whatever it was having done such a hideous and cruel thing.

Canepole spoke up."Reckon all you boys know that your mom was once a mermaid, he assurmed. "That's where you get your red hair. All mermaids are green-eyed, freckled and redheaded; helps them blend in when they surface at sunsets. I was fishing here the first time Molly showed. She came up, threw on a smile and then ducked under. I came back every evening after that. A month later, there she was. Told me, she'd give anything to have legs and a family. Don't ask how -- some things is best left a mystery -- but I'll tell you, I went and begged Moses to throw down on a heavy prayer. Without her I felt like nothing. A month later, Molly popped back up and walked out of the river and give me a kiss what's produced each and every one of you miracles. Boys, you was born to the river and fishing. There ain't nothing you can ever do about it. Whatever happens, wherever you go, you'll always be right here."

Moses thought about what Canepole was trying to do.

He was preparing for the worst in the case of Molly's dying;
preparing himself, too.

"That's as close to the truth as you'll ever hear," remarked Moses,
throwing back another drink.

A yellow butterfly with black dots and two long tails lit on the end
of his bottle as he had it tilted back and then it folded its wings. It flew
off, flittering around the head of nearly every boy before disappearing.

One of the smaller boys, Samuel, sat with his head bowed,
spellbound at the white band contrasting against the brilliant blues
along the end of a jay bird's tail feather as it twirled back and forth
while he twisted it between his thumb and finger. Momma was bad

inside his heart, too. But he didn't know what to say. Finally, the feather stopped. "Uncle Moses, are there butterflies in heaven?"

Moses looked at the boy as several heads turned to see his reaction. Differentiating between dream and reality always put a troubled nature on him. "Wouldn't be much of a heaven without one, would it?" he answered right serious. "The Bible allows that the kingdom of heaven is within you. You haven't been eating any butterflies, have ya? To be honest, when it comes to a heaven being out there somewhere, nobody knows. The ones that say they do really don't. I'm only guessing, but I believe what you see and feel right here is heaven. When chiggers eat you up or a hornet stings you or you get poison ivy -- it's all heaven. Whatever knot head allowed heaven was all clouds and angels and harps up there flying around and remembering nothing, happy all the time, like some lark never shutting up? Having everything fine all the time wouldn't be any heaven. Give that situation a long spell and it would be hell. When we disappear from this earth it doesn't mean we ain't around no more. It just means we've played out our part. Sometimes, who we were stays, maybe with someone we loved, but not always. Sometimes a soul rubs off on another. That's the best strange thing about life; generally, all we do is leave a few poor words... Butterflies in heaven...Sure, all kinds."

Seventeen peckerheads and their peckerheaded daddy and their daddy's blue-eyed, coal-haired brother sat angled amongst the spread roots staring at their reflections and still seeing the buzzard's.

Canepole looked back up at the blackest bird in the world.

31

Chapter Eight

There Ain't Nary Another-n

A-Comin' Out

Some better than a mile away from all the brothers Molly was being cared for by their sisters.

Inside the cabin there was nothing but smiles.

Molly was alive.

She had done well at having her babies this time.

Not twins, but triplets.

"That's it, there ain't nary another-n a-comin' out," assured the oldest girl, Amanda.

With that announcement, two of the fastest sisters took out the door racing for the river bursting with the news. They pounded bare footed away, scattering the chickens, cats and cows. They were almost even when they cut in between the corncrib and three outhouses.

Nancy, the less freckled of the two and a year younger, grabbed the lead but then got tripped from behind. Hopping back up, she paid no mind to her busted knee, but Kelly was already far ahead after hitting the sandy path that wove through the high weeds and down near the head of Catfish Creek.

Chapter Nine

Thank You Jesus

Down by the river Canepole's shaded face was tilted back almost to the point of his losing balance as he watched the buzzard when two cries swooped down from the sandy bank behind him.

"Pa!"

The voices were full of excitement.

"Ma's had three babies! Two of 'em is girls, and the other-n-a black-haired boy!"

"Seventeen sets of twins and now triplets," uttered Canepole, shaking his head in disbelief and rejoice.

Moses' heart stopped. "Thank you Jesus, he rejoiced."

He and his nephews raised their eyes from the emerald water and looked at Canepole who was trying to act indifferent to the news but couldn't stop the stream of tears racing down his cheeks.

Real tears.

Canepole reached in a sack pulling out a pigeon he called 'Peg Leg.' The bird had eyes redder than him and it was grey colored with black specks all over it.

He gave its head a kiss and pitched it into the air.

The boys didn't know Canepole had brought Peg Leg, but they knew the bird would go home; they sent messages like that all the time.

Of all the good times the Hawkins' had shared on the river this was the best. Moses was happy that he was there. Even happy that buzzard was still circling.

Canepole held quiet, savoring the moment. It was rare when death yawned and granted a reprieve; Rarer still to be the father of thirty-seven children.

The eater of dreams would have to go hungry.

In every way it was a liquid jade moment.

The boys relaxed into childhood again.

One of the dirty faces moved to pull out a green snake from his pocket. He untied the thing and let it wrap around his wrist and take a bite on one of his knuckles.

Another boy pulled out his knife, stood, and carved in the sycamore: "William Hawkins--JULY 11, 1836."

"PA!" The voices were still up there. "MA'S JUST HAD THREE BABIES AND--"

"YOU PECKERWOODS HESH THAT YOWL AND GIT CHEESELVES BACK HOME!" shouted Canepole. "Brother Moses," he divulged. "I feel the spirit a-comin' over me. It's time for us to crack that Bible of yorn."

Moses hoped Canepole would hold up for another little taste before trotting off back to the cabin.

Moses looked down at his Bible.

It was the biggest and most ragged edition on earth having always served as a seat when fishing and when fighting, a weapon. "What chapter would you like?" he entreated.

"The middle-n," avowed Canepole.

"That's the same verse I like," joked Moses, opening his Bible; withdrawing a bottle from its carved out pages, revealing Moses' true nature as a real spiritual leader more than some Ezekiel.

"What verse do you best like?" asked Canepole.

"Why Cane," answered Moses in a tone of disbelief. "The Lord helps them what help themselves.'"

Chapter Ten

Freckled Legs

Up from the river stood the Hawkins' log cabin, built of solid chestnut, it lay somber in the green and peaceful embrace of cedar, pine and hemlock.

Entering through its only door, which formed a square hole in the cabin's middle, the two returned sisters from the river ran over to where all their sisters were huddled.

Prying through a canebrake of pale, freckled legs, they stopped at Molly's bedside.

"We told dad, Mom, but he didn't say nothing. He hollered and told us to get back home. You ain't had no more babies, have ya?" Molly normally kept her thick mane perfectly combed and parted in the middle but not after the ordeal she had been through. In her even featured and freckled face were green eyes that could feel but not see; she had been born that way. The eyes looked like they could see but they couldn't. Even now, for all her children, she was that safety cluck of a mother grouse. She smiled towards the two flushed faces that were panting and itching for a response. Without responding a word she brought her face back down at the healthy baby in her arms; he had blue eyes and long eyelashes; such high cheeks and thick eyebrows; somehow, they were a

Kentucky mountain ridge. "He's the most beautiful child I've ever had," she spoke, lightly rubbing her hands over the baby's face. "He's beautiful like a dream," she insisted, handing her baby over to a pair of anxious hands that were waiting to wrap him up. "He's my sinful miracle," she stated, remaining smileful.

"He's got a birthmark on his belly," noticed Nancy.

Molly smiled. "He's an angel," she said, letting go of his tiny grasping hands.

"Lo-rd," said one of the older girls, holding a fixed stare on the baby's male membership. "Little Ed'ard here jes' might out-do Uncle Moses -- he's sure got the equipment!" If there was one thing The Reverend Moses was known for all over Estill County, it wasn't preaching.

"Good," remarked Molly. "We could definitely use another preacher in the family."

Alone, hollow-boned, the winged serpent flew.

So very high.

So unnoticed.

Waiting.

Chapter Eleven

Some Years Later Down By the

Same Old Sycamore

Ah-h, the shade of a sycamore and the company of a solid fishing friend: And of all things, discussing the merits of one's poor old pet pigeon.

"Peg Leg's mate laid three eggs," allowed Canepole, passing his small brown jug over to Huby, Irvine's part time turkey hunting guide and full time drunk. "Pigeons always lay two white eggs. But on this last go around, Peg Leg's mate laid three. If memory serves, that makes thirty-seven babies for that pigeon. That happens to be my number, too. That last baby of Peg Leg's ain't nothing like the others he's had, this-n is all black feathers with blue eyes. Reminds me some of Ed. Nary hawk can catch that bird. You'd swear his daddy was a gamecock."

Huby smiled and flopped over.

"Whiskey flows through me worser than the river does through Kentucky," he mumbled, adding, "With flooding more often."

He laid there with a root for a pillow while the sun wasted itself beaming down onto his round face attempting to soothe his tortured soul.

Canepole was just fixing to tell his whiskered companion how Peg Leg had gotten his name; about that bird getting caught in a trap and limping for a year.

But as Canepole observed the mess of mankind now beside him, passed out and snoring, he realized his words would be wasted.

That moonshine you create and sell to the Judge and then the Judge sells back to Irvine doesn't help anything, except dying, he thought, if you could cross a bear with a muskrat that would be you. Whatever you are you are one hundred per cent Irvine, Kentucky. God bless your little heart.

Canepole kept looking at the river.

"I wish that during the past seven years me and Molly had had three more babies," he declared, knowing that he was talking aloud to himself. "That would have made an even forty. There's something religious about that forty number; It rained for forty days and forty nights before Noah pitched anchor. For forty days and nights, Moses stayed up on that mountain chewing the fat and getting God's laws. For forty years, Moses wandered all over the place before his bunch found the promise land. Jonah told that bunch in that wicked city they had to behave for forty days or the Lord was going to thump 'em. Goliath took and beat on his chest for forty days before little David took and slung that rock. And Jesus, he never had no drank for forty days and nights out there in that wilderness while the devil was a-temptin' on him with red liquor and everything; poor feller, bound to have gotten the shakes. And Jesus, his bunch kept on seeing him on earth for forty days, following-up after that crucifixion stuff."

Yeah, forty.

But forty never got there for Canepole.

Times drifted by and for the most part Peg Leg never saw much of his babies. Old pigeons always got to a point in their lives where they no longer recognized their offspring. For them that might have been alright. But for Canepole, well, he never wanted to reach that predicament. Without his children he felt like nothing. Both his and that pigeon's offspring had somehow disappeared; some survived along the cliffs near the river. But for many, they were just gone. Gone where, neither knew. It had been impossible for all thirty-seven Hawkins children to stay together.

Things wild have to be what they are or they ain't nothing.

Chapter Twelve

Growin' Up

"Don't you lie to me, Edward Hawkins, I know you did it!" warned Molly, back from a revival as she placed her straw bonnet on a table; Nailed on the wall above the table, framed for her family, was her own red hair that had been boiled and woven into the image of a large rose.

Ed's opiate blue eyes peered up.

"Do what?" he challenged, knowing that he was able to control his world with that curl in his upper lip, especially when combined with any of the dimples he held in reserve. The light from the doorway was shining on his duck-tailed, black hair, one of his features promoting his pride.

Molly listened to the tone of Ed's voice. She knew more about Ed than she could ever say. "What am I going to do with you? You know full well what I am talking on, your father's Jew's harp. The one he's been taking fishing lately."

"He done it, mom," ratted William. "He's just acting. You know how he is!"

"Will's a liar! He's the one that took it! He's trying to lay it on me!"

"Son, you know how I don't like that word, liar. Shows you ain't got no manners. There'll come a day when you're judged on your manners. People like somebody that's nice."

"But Mom…"

Molly moved her hands through the air and stepped over to the fireplace, fooling around to light her stemmed pipe. "Boys, lying and stealing will put you in the devil's pit. You know how hot the skillet gets? Well, the devil's fire is forty times worser."

Chapter Thirteen

The Shadow of Your Smile

The morning after the Jew's harp disappearance Canepole lay in his bed loudly snoring, recuperating from another of his drunken fishing exploits. Peg Leg was just perking up and starting to coo and strut to a little hen close by when a squall busted loose down under inside in the cabin.

After Canepole's bleary eyes straightened some, he saw Molly standing by her favorite possession, a rocking chair; the one that he'd made for her as a wedding gift; covering the headboard of the rocker was the fresh and bold carving: "WILL."

Everyone knew that Will had recently bought a pocket knife; A destruction of this nefarious nature needed severe punishment.

The evidence pointed to Will.

But everyone knew better.

And the only one not around was Ed.

"You know what freckles are?" announced Molly, gathering herself, looking back at to where she thought was her family. "They're luck. I'm the luckiest woman that ever lived. Every time I'm near my family, I smell wild flowers. Funny how something I've never seen, the sun,

47

makes them bloom. And, you know, red heads smell sweet. Heaven is right here, alright. There's no supposing that."

Molly always had a way of holding Canepole's heart.

What a woman.

"Honey," he said, watching her run her hands over the carving, "I'll make you a new head board."

"No. I wouldn't take anything for this one."

That afternoon, Ed found himself alone at his hideout, a cane break surrounding a sycamore near Catfish Creek.

Ed had made a low path through the canes that only a fox could follow that led over the hill to the river.

He was stretched back against the bank when two poles began nodding. Catfish, he thought.

Lost in the river's whispers, he felt content.

No matter the configuration of his blood, he was all Hawkins.

Life ain't too bad, he observed, seeing his poles bend further into the water, as long as you've got a story.

Chapter Fourteen

Twelve Year Old Ed and Moses at the

Hideout

Entwined with the enchanting smell of Moses' kif cigar, his voice floated through the sycamore shade with a tinkling of truth far more precious than the holy whisper of the river. "You've got to be an actor," he drawled, rearranging a deuce in his fantailed hand, "Before you can nefariate anyone."

Until now, nobody had ever been invited to Ed's hideout.

Ed smiled, holding a hand full of face cards.

"SNAKE!" hollered Moses, eyeing behind Ed.

Ed froze.

He wasn't scared of a snake if he got to see it first.

He turned around, seeing nothing except a stick in the sand. Turning back around he noticed the disappearance of a button; one he'd been using in place of money.

"Uncle Moses, if you tricked a feller and he caught you, would you confess?"

"Son, never confess to nothing. All it does is prove ignorance. A confession might be good for the soul but it's awful on the body. Always have a story. And always stick to it. A smart liar can go a long ways. Look at all the politicians."

Ed took his eyes off the remaining buttons and looked back over into Moses' same hypnotic blue eyes that he owned himself. "What's nefarious mean?" he asked; that word had been bothering him for some time.

Moses blew a smoke ring.

"That word is a bunch of things," he claimed. "The first time I saw it was when a Bible fell open. I never thought much more about that word and then a week later, I heard an important preacher using it. After his sermon the word brought him in a bucket of cash. I thought, hmm, if that word can make money like that, maybe I ought to use it. From then on, me and that word have been partners. Let's quit—you win," he conceded, folding his cards, lying back against the ground, yawning, shutting his eyes. "Play me some of that Jew's harp."

Rising, Ed eased back up through his path to his look out station, the sycamore. About ten feet up in the tree was a horseshoe. Lightning had once struck the shoe creating a split-out in the tree creating Ed's hiding spot. Going back through the path with his Jew's harp he sat down beside Moses. "I'll play us something if you'll tell me who Duke is," he offered, withdrawing a silver flask.

Moses cracked an eye.

Then both eyes opened.

Ed was rubbing and polishing the flask against his pants. The word: "DUKE" was engraved on the flask's side.

Moses was surprised that Canepole had allowed such a possession to somehow escape.

"Isn't that the flask I once gave your dad?"

"He lost it back many years ago."

"I see that. Well, least it's still in the family."

Moses felt special about Ed entrusting him. There was nobody on earth he wanted to be entrusted by more.

"Are you willing to tell me who Duke is? Or do I have to drink all of this by myself?"

"Duke is a Lord," informed Moses, "The Lord of Ink."

"The Lord of what?"

"Ink, as in the green kind married to money."

Ed looked at Moses staring at the flask. "I'll bet Duke is nefarious," he commented.

Moses released another smoke ring.

Ed's voice had changed since he'd last paid a visit. Somewhere, the boy in that voice was fast disappearing. He had developed into a lad you enjoyed being near, good-looking, inquisitive and funny.

Over the past dozen years Moses had been checking on Ed, teaching him how to shoot, skin a deer, sport manners and do all sorts of things important in surviving. "Bring that silver darling over here," he implored. "Let's have a little taste."

Ed held back a grin, acting like he wasn't going to give Moses a drink, teasing, moving the flask towards him and then jerking it back. He opened the top and smelled its contents. "Wonder what's in there?"

"Tonic: Heaven's gateway."

Ed throwdback "Wow!" he shouted; his young innards were on fire.

"Getting to heaven is rough, ain't it?" informed Moses. He took the flask and finished it off. "Hell or heaven," he deduced, "Makes no difference—it's the ride that counts."

Side by side, Ed and Moses breathed in rhythm; they laid face up toward a blue sky for the longest time; the sand felt perfect. Both wondered what was beyond the sky.

"Uncle Moses, is heaven really out there?"

"A lot of folk sure think so."

"Uncle Moses."

"Yes?"

"When I die, I'd like to go to heaven. But I don't know. I'm not sure I want to float around, forever."

"There's lots of heavens, son. But real heaven is a loving heart aimed in your direction."

"It is?"

"Absolutely, and if you want heaven, I can help."

"You can?"

"Yep, that is, when you're in command of fifty dollars."

"FIFTY DOLLARS!"

"Heaven isn't cheap. If it were, the streets wouldn't be gold. You can't expect to pass through the pearly gates for nothing."

"Where is this Fifty Dollar Heaven?"

"One Ninety Four North Upper Street; in the city of fast horses and faster women—Lexington. A place called, The Eagle's Nest: Miss Chesteen's Home for the Lost and Misdirected."

"Is The Eagle's Nest, really heaven?"

"All the heaven you'll ever want."

Ed and Moses continued lying on the ground, breathing slow and easy, feeling the earth's pull, watching a bird circling so high that was almost nothing.

"Ever hear of a game called 'grab'?"

"No?"

"In the event a signet ring can't be employed to reflect our cards, it's where we go to plan B."

"Plan B—'Grab'. That's where we wait at the right time when all the money is on the table and then I'll insult whoever I'm playing in such a way as to develop a sure fight. Now, when the fists commence to flyin', that's when you commence to grabbin'. Immediately after you've high-tailed with all the money, I'll act ruined over the tragedy. Cry. Allow what you grabbed was my precious foundation money left unto me by my Christian grandmother. I'll mourn so sad that all the turtle doves in Kentucky won't have nothing to do for a year. And for safe measure, I'll take me a fit. A good fit is worth its weight in gold: Hoot. Holler. Speak in tongue. Scratch. Snort. Spit. Hiss. Gasp. Cough. Roll. Bark. Chant... Son, all the world is a stage, the best actor gets the spoils."

Ed could see it. Yeah. Grab. Grabbin' with Uncle Moses, and maybe, visiting heaven. "But what if there's a gun?"

"Never need you worry, son. Guns happen to be one of my spesheealities. I can smell a musket a mile away, pistols, m-m-m, about half that, depending on the wind. Any gun within a hundred foot, I'll tell you what type, how well it's been treated, if it's stolen and whether or not it's ever been or ever even likely to have been, fired at a man."

Chapter Fifteen

Leaving Home For the Big City

As Moses and Ed walked through the woods Moses would stop
and ask Ed if he recognized certain sounds. They would stand silent
for a moment and then Ed would tell him that it was a little woodpeck-
er or one of the big red headed woodpeckers that they sometimes shot
and ate and called wood hens. They would hear a squirrel bark and
then soon there would be squirrels all throughout the woods barking
and telling the other squirrels that danger in the form of two intrud-
ers was near. At one point, Moses grabbed Ed's arm and told him to
be quiet. A few seconds later an immense flock of blackbirds broke
out over the mountains directly above their heads with such a rushing of wings that it stopped both of their hearts. Both had had many
experiences in the woods but never before had they encountered such
a powerful noise from the sky. They watched the birds quickly disappear and for that moment they were as close as two men could ever
be. "You'll be on this earth a long time after I am gone," spoke Moses.
"I'll leave you my stories, my blood and everything I own—from there
it'll be up to you to wade through the mess of mankind."

Chapter Sixteen

Miss Chesteen's String of Pearls

"A man comes and goes in and out of this world alone, but as long as he's an outlaw, he's always got company," assured Moses, flipping cigar ashes, looking past a wet, wrought iron fence surrounding the finest brick cathouse in Kentucky and the willows in front of it.

Ed took a throwback, finishing off his flask. His new boots had his feet begging for air. Behind the willows rose an ivy covered mansion with glowing stained windows.

"Give me the money," spoke Moses. "Only a fool enters a cathouse with good cash."

"What are you going to do with it?" asked Ed, handing over one hundred dollars, reward from the previous evening's game of 'grab'.

"Hide it right here," answered Moses, lifting a flat rock, "Where the Lord and me can save it from the devil."

"But won't we need money?"

"Yeah, but not cash-good-money, here, take this."

Ed watched as Moses reached into his white suit pulling out a Shawnee pouch. "What's that?" he asked.

"Fifty dollars of Duke's finest: Art, my desperate last."

All Ed had heard that afternoon from Moses was how God had spoken unto him relaying they should first proceed to the tenderloin tippling house of Miss Chesteen's. After that, hit Louisville. Duke's soul needed checking on. And his exchange rate for cash-good-money did, too.

"Well," spoke Moses, egging Ed, "Are you ready for heaven?"

A minute later, Ed's gloved hand took hold on a brass, rooster head knocker. Gulping, two strokes were pounded.

Opening the door stood a flock of freckles with exquisite red hair, Miss Chesteen; she was dressed in black lace and wearing a string of irregular shaped, purplish pearls; off behind her, stood an Imari vase with a peacock painted on it.

"Moses," she said, embracing his advance. "Come in, you missed last Saturday. I was afraid that giant catfish got you."

Ed grinned.

Miss Chesteen grinned back. "I suppose you know all about that catfish?" she asked, looking at Ed.

Ed continued smiling.

He could see that in between each of Miss Chesteen's river pearls were beads of polished black, yellow and red agate. "They tell the catfish is pale yellow and bigger than six bulls."

"Moses, who is this handsome devil you've brought me?"

"My nephew, Ed, he's on loan for assistation in fighting the devil. Today, the unfortunate lamb turned thirteen. As you know, thirteen is an unlucky number. He bad needs a powerful change on his luck. A transformation you can possibly help with, if you get my meaning."

Miss Chesteen kept her sparkling green eyes on Ed. Remarkable, she thought, Moses all over again. "This being the most orderly of disorderly houses, I believe that I can arrange for this 'luck transformation,'" she promised, "But it's going to cost twenty dollars for all night: Straight cash. Good money: In advance. And that doesn't include your own wish."

"My wish, you know what my wish is and always will be—you. You are all my dreams in one."

"Then, it'll be fifty dollars. A dollar for every year of your age and don't think I don't know it!"

"Lord God, that's an awful lot. Fifty, I'm not that old, am I?"

"It'll be the best money you'll ever spend."

"Pay her, Ed. Miss Chesteen never lies."

As Ed handed Miss Chesteen their money he saw a parrot perched near the ceiling.

"If this is bad money, then it's the best bad money I've ever seen," quipped Miss Chesteen, counting. "I'm thinking about changing the name of my place to 'The Parrot House'. God knows, there's been more parrots roost here than eagles. That's why men of your distinction are always welcome."

Moses looked into Miss Chesteen's hemp-green eyes. "Miss Chesteen," he beamed. "You can sure lay on a line."

"For the right cash, I can lay on anything."

"There's a purdy gal," hollered the parrot, observing Miss Chesteen.

Following Miss Chesteen through a Brussels carpeted cherry hallway, Ed and Moses saw massive furniture, rich bookcases and soft, spacious rooms leading in every direction.

In one room, fine gold leaf pier mirrors reflected cathedral-like stained glass windows that were glowing from the lights of numerous red oil lamps as some angel continue playing the piano. From upstairs there was periodic laughter.

"Would you care for a bottle of champagne?" inquired Miss Chesteen as they arrived at the parlor. "My champagne is like my girls, firm, but yielding to men of good taste."

"Champagne's good for the soul, eh Ed?"

Ed looked at Moses. He didn't know beans about champagne. "Two bottles of your most nefarious," he ordered.

"And would you care for some fresh, spiced Baltimore oysters?"

"All you can carry, darling."

Sitting down into chairs made of stretched leopard skin and longhorns, Ed and Moses watched as Miss Chesteen departed.

Between their chairs laid a white wolf rug with a mean face. In the center of the room was a cherry table partially covered in lace; on the lace, causing rainbows was the finest of silver and cut glass. At each end of the mantel where Ed and Moses were relaxing and flipping their ashes in silver cuspidors, fine ladies in silks and imported laces kept easing around the doorway, until finally in promenaded Miss Chesteen carrying a silver tray mounded in ice and oysters. Behind her followed a yellow skinned girl owning long hair in lots of tight braids; she was wearing a black Zouave jacket and carrying two bottles and four glasses.

"Ed," introduced Miss Chesteen, "I'd like for you to meet Jasmine. In Charleston, she fetched two thousand in gold. Her father was the governor of Virginia. Tonight, she's yours. It's her first time to be with anyone. If breathes a lady that can affect your luck, it's her."

Chapter Seventeen

A Kiss to Build a Dream On

After two days of touring Kentucky's fabulous hole in the ground, the biggest hole in the world, the famed Mammoth Cave, and gawking at the torch-lit images of the upside down posture of many a small, brown and long-eared bat what scared the holy hell out of her, Miss Jenny Lind, the young and famous "Swedish Nightingale," and her traveling companion, the reticent Josephine Giovanni, were met ten miles outside of Louisville by a delirious coach load of esteemed citizens, the bloated political Shakers and Movers of the State, imbued with the spirit of adventure, expert in the art of genuflection; liars par excellence; Four magnificent, black thoroughbreds and four stately, black, hat-tipping coachmen were then mounted to her carriage.

As Jenny's coach journeyed toward Louisville, it drew close to two slumped humble figures hoeing turnips in their field. "Oh-h-h," one of them sighed, momentarily pausing, straightening her back, wiping sweat, reaching to her neck and fondling her one treasure, a small pewter cross. "If only the Lord would let me hear the Nightingale."

To hear Jenny sing was billed as the ultimate religious experience, uplifting and purifying the soul to such an extent that nothing was ever the same. Amen.

She was charity, simplicity and goodness personified.

For two months, every person from the most remote hollow in eastern Kentucky to the governor's mansion had been anticipating the world's most powerful and delicate soprano voice, a direct angel from the softest cloud in heaven coming to Kentucky to sing, "The Last Rose of Summer."

"Look at all the church spires," spoke Jenny, gazing toward the outskirts of Louisville's skyline. "I'm astonished that such a large city be so near the wilderness."

"Yonder be the Anne T.!" shouted a voice, just as Jenny's carriage hit a deep rut, came out of that rut, and again back into another. Along the road and running alongside the wide Ohio, were many docked rafts of logs and majestic sternwheelers; on their cluttered decks were stacked bales of cotton, barrels of whiskey, chopped wood, turkeys and chickens, hogs, horses and slaves that were chained six and six together.

Coming onto the finest and widest boulevard in Louisville, an active city experiencing a colorful, rambunctious interlude of advancement because of its strategic location as a river-rail crossing in the great westward push, Jenny began to lightly bounce as her carriage absorbed the bricked street on the northeast corner of Second and Main. Rows of pin oak trees were seen flanking substantial houses, many having galleries around their upper stories with steep outside ladders leading up from their neat fronts and airy back gardens. Many elaborate carriages holding proud figures in tall hats and shaded figures beneath parasols were being drawn by staunch animals bred-exact for the moment. "It's like being in Paris," spoke Jenny as her carriage proceeded. A curtain blew through one open window, while at another with eyes in-study, children pressed their noses. A wagon was unloading at one curb. And a carriage, attended by a black footman in the finest livery, waited near a large sign: "Bent & Duvall."

Drawing closer, one hundred marching firemen clad in scarlet woolen shirts and proudly holding lit torches fell in behind Jenny's carriage; large flags were draped out many windows. Melancholia filled the air as The Louisville Musical Society serenaded their version of "Weep No More My Lady."

Halting in front of the Galt House, an impressive five-story hotel taking up an entire city square, the carriage's door opened. "MAKE WAY! MAKE WAY! MISS JENNY LIND! MAKE WAY!" A deep, black voice kept sterning the crowd. "MAKE WAY! MAKE WAY!"

A bugle iced the air as children, each with a red rose, stepped forth giving a sweet speech and a kiss on Jenny's cheek. Each child left dazzled, having touched the Nightingale.

A round, robust, red-faced man with black, wild curly hair and powerful outstretched arms stood beside Jenny. "MY DEAR, GOOD FRIENDS," he shouted. "YOU HAVE OFTEN HEARD IT ASKED, 'WHERE IS MR. P.T. BARNUM? WHERE IS THE MAN WHO CAN BRING US CULTURE?' 'WHERE IS THE MAN THAT SACRIFICED ALL HE OWNS TO GIVE YOU A MOMENT IN HEAVEN?' NOW, NOW AT LAST, YOU WELL MAY SAY, HE IS HERE!"

Louisville roared with a cheer.

"MISS LIND'S SHARE OF TONIGHT'S CONCERT IS TWENTY-FIVE THOUSAND DOLLARS-ALL OF WHICH SHE'LL BE GIVING AWAY TO THE ORPHANS, THE DESTITUTE, THE FRIENDLESS, THE INDIGENT, THE PROTESTANT, THE ROMAN CATHOLIC, THE FIRE BRIGADE, THE LOUISVILLE HISTORICAL, CULTURAL AND MUSICAL FUND SOCIETIES!"

Again, the crowd broke loose with a maddening cheer.

Under a huge cloud of colorful, swirling, wing-whistling pigeons, they caterwauled, clapped, cart wheeled, body-flipped, beat drums, tossed hats, smashed bottles, threw flowers, fired guns, picked up loose aces, war hooped, pinched ladies, blew horns, backhanded slaves, kicked dogs, slung babies, belched, bellered, pick-pocketed and finished-off mint-jammed juleps.

"I KNOW THAT MY REDEEMER LIVETH!" declared Jenny. Then, she left, following her manager, Mr. Barnum, the man who had sacrificed his entire fortune, gambling she'd make him a success.

Upon entering the hotel, Jenny and her entourage passed under three massive arches supported by eight 18 foot hand-fluted Corinthian columns. It was cool inside, remindful of the way Mammoth Cave had been; the thick outside walls of the Galt House were made of large gray bricks formed from hand burnt shale which absorbed the day's noises and heat.

The promenade entrance opened into a rotunda that was sixty-six feet in diameter made entirely of pink marble, with paintings and bas-reliefs of the greatest costs.

At the opposite end of the rotunda, obedient slaves in white gloves, aprons and snug-fitting jackets, carried baskets containing pyramids of fruits. In front of the slaves, nervously shifting his bulky weight from one foot to the other, was the new and congenial governor of Kentucky, a beleaguered, well-dressed man owning a gaze of insanity; tossed strands of white hair were slicked down, trying to hide his war-weary, bald forehead; John Crittenden, the former governor, had recently resigned his office to become the United States Attorney General under President Fillmore.

Chapter Eighteen

A Keg of Tar and a Blind Mule

Upstairs in the Galt House, on the fifth and top floor in The Isaac Shelby Suite, in an opulent roost located just under a giant American flag advertising thirty stars, sat Moses and Duke, wry eyeing each other in a high game of draw poker. For the past two years, they, along with Ed, had been, well, nefarious. On their polished, cherry table, were two .44 caliber Baby Dragoons, two gold watches, two near-empty glasses, two lit cigars, an unlit candle and a quart of bourbon resting on top of Moses' Bible.

Behind Moses, lay Ed, resting on a brass feather bed.

A small chandelier hung over his crossed bare feet as he sat partially up reading Louisville's newspaper, The Daily Courier:

"The Newest Princess of the Foot lit Realm: Miss Jenny Lind."

On the nightstand near Ed's head, rested a Jew's harp, lit cigar, silver flask, a small silver container and a tight roll of counterfeit.

"I'll ante two paid nights at The Eagle's Nest," issued Moses, "July Fourth and New Year's."

"I'm upping the pot one cotton plantation and three sternwheelers."

67

"I'll go you, the city of Richmond."

"I'll see you with Irvine, and call you."

"Reverend, Irvine isn't capital near enough. Any fool knows that."

"I'll take the wager back and substitute Irvine for a keg of tar and a blind mule."

"That'll do. But don't ever try to ring Irvine in on me again. I'm a gentleman. I must have everything fair and honest."

"Fair and honest," rebuked Moses, laying down four aces and the wildcard joker. "There are you five fair and honest aces," he delivered.

Duke looked at Moses' cards. "It's a draw," he declared, showing no emotion, laying down his hand, also four aces and a wildcard joker.

"You haven't changed one hair over the years, have you?" concluded Moses, reaching for his drink.

Duke lifted his glass, studying its dark whiskey against the light from the window. "You could say, I'm still touched with insanity, corrupted with lust and still nefariously stimulated by bourbon."

Moses turned and looked at Ed. "Do you see anything on who's coming to see our high chirping Miss Lind?"

Ed brought the newspaper up to his face. "AUGUST 23, 1851— THE NIGHTINGALE SINGS TONIGHT," he read.

After stopping a moment to read to himself, he continued. "She's twenty-nine years old. When she leaves Louisville, she's headed for Boston: Going to marry Otto Goldschmidt; A composer and pianist... He's seven years younger than her."

Moses loved listening to Ed; the education he'd given him went beyond mere school. "Likes her beaus younger, huh? That could work to our advantage."

Ed continued reading and then gave another report…

"There's a ten point contract between Jenny and P.T. I've never seen such a bunch of greedy words thrown together. P.T. fronted her $187,000 to come to America. Promised to pay for anything she desired: The best hotels; the best transportation; whatever she wants to eat: protection, clothes. You name it."

Duke eased over to a tall corner window, looking down at the fashionable flock gathered below. Off past the city, he could see the wide Ohio River and a churning steamer. He had already studied the newspaper, and saw the story explaining why the Nightingale had journeyed by carriage instead of boat. She would rather break down than blow up. Also, she owned an overwhelming fear of snakes. There was no way she'd expose herself to all the "river pythons hanging loose between Mammoth Cave and The Galt House."

"It says here," continued Ed, "That Henry Clay, Daniel Webster, Horace Greely, Charles Dickens, John Whittier, Ralph Emerson, Nathaniel Hawthorne, Walt Whitman, James Lowell, Louis Agassiz, John Audubon, Charles Baudelaire, Stephen Foster, and—"

"That's sure a lot of money," drawled Moses, interrupting, owning a queer dream look. Gazing down, his face kept staring at the oriental design gracing the rug.

Duke struck a match. "Isn't the story on her, that some queen heard her trolling to a cat and then that queen became overcome? And shortly after, overcame Barnum, 'Mr. Shakespeare of Advertising,' specializing in freaks and fakes and all the curiosity and culture that a body can afford."

"I heard tale, the queen heard singing one midnight and tore into the king's room and there was Jenny, naked and none sober."

"It says here, Miss Lind should receive over twenty-five thousand dollars for singing one song," spoke Ed, still buried in the newspaper.

"Su-ur-re a lot of money," repeated Moses, lost in some luxuriant dream.

"It sure is," agreed Duke, butting his black cigar. "And not," he confided, while inspecting his manicured fingers, "The sort that leaves ink on your hands."

"I'd give anything to see Miss Lind," marveled Ed, as he languished the thought. He laid his newspaper over his chest and stared at the chandelier. "She's all my dreams in one," he admitted.

"Lamb," advised Moses, "Miss Jenny is all our dreams in one: Her and all her money."

"How much treasure do you suppose our Nightingale keeps tucked away in her roost?" entreated Duke, sitting down, refilling his glass.

"It's got to be right smart. Little Jenny has been warbling that ruby throat all over the country. If she hasn't deposited her money in a scattered covey of banks, come late tonight, her room ought to be heaven. You know, that 'P' and 'T' in

Barnum's name must stand for possum and treasure. Ed, hand me the ink and paper. You wanted to see Jenny, didn't you?"

Chapter Nineteen

The Truth in a Nut Keg

"God, I love birds, especially nightingales," spoke Moses.

He dipped a quill.

"The Lord moves in a mysterious way," he preached, "And sometimes, he moves ink mysteriously upon paper."

"Like the Bible?"

"Ed," reassured Duke, "God created the heavens, the earth, giant catfish and a whole bunch of stuff. He quit after six days. Realized that everything he'd made was nothing but one awful mistake. God ain't hit a lick since. If he was still in production, we might call on him for help. But he ain't. And that's why brave men like us have to take his powers and put them in our hands."

"That's the truth in a nut keg," disclosed Moses.

Taking the time to write in the most elegant of style, as though some Trappist monk reincarnated, he composed the following:

Isaac Shelby Suite
Galt House

August 23, 1851

Dear Miss Lind,

My heart tells me that you must be God's dearest angel and I am praying that you will come tonight and visit a child that I don't believe will live to see the morning. My young friend's name is Edward W. Crittenden, our former governor's only child. He has been extremely ill for the longest of time. We had hoped that he might be able to see you perform tonight as you are all his dreams in one, but such was not the case.

Please, as a dying child's last wish, a moment of relief in the lamb's darkest hour, I beseech you to come and see him.

In Prayer,
Rev. Moses Hawkins

P.S. There could be a good deal of money in this for you if you come now with the doctor.

Ed leaned over Moses' shoulder, observing as fancy curlicues were being added. "What malady am I dying of?" he begged, looking innocent.

"Decay child, tertiary decay of the absolute and most nefarious variety."

"How did I get it?"

"Somehow, it grabbed you when your poor snake bit mother killed over."

"Do you believe there's any chance that I might live the night through?"

"Only if God heeds my prayers."

Duke flipped his ashes. "And only," he added, nestled in front of a mirror, preening his sharp features, "If Doctor Duke's tonic takes hold."

Ed watched Duke comb his black hair and dab lilac water on the back of his neck. "Tonic?" he asked.

"Yes," acknowledged Duke, winking, gently patting the flask inside his coat. "And also," he informed, looking at the silver container on the nightstand, "the vapors."

"Yea, verily yea," voiced Moses, straightening his robe, lifting his Bible, "Them heavenly vapors."

Chapter Twenty

Hummingbird

Somewhere beyond the smoke-filled Galt House rookery of plotting human peregrines drowning their gullets in bourbon, beyond the lovely laud of a Nightingale enriching P. T.'s pockets, beyond countless church spires pin cushioning clouds and directing north bound souls on nimbus paths to heaven, beyond the marvelous and maddening flock of intoxicant civilization and all of its high priced culture, somewhere in the soft distance along the river bottom there was a soft field of flowering hemp; a remarkable, purple field consisting solely of virginal female plants.

Appearing and disappearing along the tops of the plants, there was a low, singular buzzing; a feathered ruby; a hummingbird, not much bigger than a June bug.

It darted with unique grace and paused in mid-air, dipping its head, poking its tongue, sampling the narcotic nectar of sappy, swollen buds, playing hummer tag from plant to plant in uncommon delight. Feeling ruby content, it vanished to the edge of the field, landing ever so light in a sycamore; on the end of a branch extending out over the water.

It sat next to a large, lime-colored leaf for a moment, and then, suddenly, its sweet world changed.

Its little head became a mess:

Its needle beak seemed to stretch across the river.

Its wings felt unflappable and ponderous.

It leaped out from its limb only to fall, flutter and splash head-on into the cool, consuming water.

The hummer began emitting small, expanding circles in the water while struggling for the close shore.

"Splash," Its mite wings pranced upon the water as if some Jesus walking-on-water, water bug.

"Splash," It continued flopping, straining, and getting closer to shore.

"SPLASH!"

Suddenly, there was only silence. The hummer, as if a lost dream, was gone.

A leaf seesawed down from the sycamore, landing and floating upon the water.

A frog broke the surface, blink-peeping at shore.

And a golden bass, a few feathers heavier than it had been moments earlier, swam ruby content back to deeper water.

Chapter Twenty One

Tonic and Vapors

Not long after Jenny Lind's famous song, "The Last Rose of Summer," had been seraphically warbled and the utmost tenacious of her admirers artfully ushered away, there came a gloved tapping upon her fancy door. "Miss Lind," introduced Duke, looking Atlantis deep into aroused dark eyes, "I am Doctor Basil Rathbone Duke, personal physician to our—may he rest in peace—former governor. I am sorry to disturb you at this late hour, but a child's life hangs in the balance."

Having been the one to have opened the door, Miss Josephine Giovanni's virginal loins began to grow warm; before her was her Eros. "I am-a-no Miss Jenny Lind," she stammered. "But I will-a-go-get the signora."

Overhearing the conversation, Jenny finished her glass of warm milk and entered the room; she stood by Josephine, further opening the door.

"I am Jenny Lind," she informed, seeing Duke. "Please, come in. How may I help? A child's life, you say?"

Duke watched as Jenny's eyes roamed over his tall frame.

Behind Josephine, off through another door, he spotted an ornate chest at the foot of a canopy bed.

"Miss Lind, Ma'am," he consoled, "I have an urgent letter from the good Reverend Moses for you."

Jenny's dainty hand took the letter. She read to herself, moving her lips, absorbing the words. Lowering the letter, she looked up into Duke's brown eyes. "Will you please take me to the child?" she urged.

"The Reverend has been praying all evening that you wouldn't be too important to understand," responded Duke, hastening the gals, shutting the door with his articulate touch.

Signaling with four low knocks, Duke tapped the walnut door of the Isaac Shelby Suite; behind him, stood the worried faces of Jenny and Josephine.

The door opened and there stood the doleful, red-eyed Reverend Moses, wearing his black velvet robe, clutching his Bible; from the room, came a pungent odor as if wet hay were on fire.

"Any change in his condition," whispered Duke, poking his head inside the dim-lit room.

"None," reported Moses; looking down with grief, he invited everyone in with a slow swoop of his Bible.

Duke tip-toed over to the bed, sitting down next to where Ed was under the covers, sleeping; he placed his hand to Ed's forehead and shook his head sideways in defeat.

"Has he much longer?" implored Jenny.

"I'm afraid the child hasn't long," he despaired. "He could go at any moment."

Standing on the other side of the bed, Moses was wiping tears from his face, switching hands with his Bible, looking down, gazing as though into his own grave. "The poor lamb is as weak as water," he conceded.

Pulling the covers down to expose Ed's lean chest, Duke paused, checked his gold watch, and then, laid his head against Ed's heart, shutting his eyes. After a minute, he opened his eyes, raised, re-checked his watch and noted that it was midnight. "He must have my tonic and vapors if he's to survive another hour." Reaching inside his coat he withdrew a silver flask.

"Decay," pined Moses, clutching his Bible. "Tertiary decay," he proclaimed, weeping. "Of the absolute and most nefarious variety," he accepted, lowering his Bible, handing Duke an empty glass.

Filling the glass, Duke set the clear tonic on top of the nightstand. Bending over, he felt under the bed, retrieving a hedge apple.

"What's that?" implored Jenny.

"Sssh-h-h-h," whispered Duke. In the center of the hedge apple, he cut out a hole causing a sticky white liquid to emit. "The slightest disturbance could send the child into the great nowhere," he cautioned. "We're lucky," he added, "Tonight, there's a full moon." Taking the glass, he poured the clear liquid into the hedge apple. "Normally, this preparation is used to ward off autumnal fever," he stated, shaking his head. "If only his mother hadn't—"

"Yea," interrupted Moses, "That demon snake."

"Miss Lind," briefed Duke, "Edward's poor mother—may the angels cherish her beauty—was attacked and bit by a 13 foot river rattler. She passed away last month."

"To everything there's a season," quoted Moses.

"He's not eaten since," relayed Duke. "His mother was his whole world."

"All his days he eateth in darkness," summated Moses. Duke handed Jenny the hedge apple. "Miss Jenny," he proposed, "Will you try to get the boy to take my tonic? He might take it from you. You are all his dreams in one."

"Give strong drink unto him that's a-fixin' to perish," decreed Moses.

Ed stirred. "M-muh-mother," he stuttered. "M-Mother," he repeated, rearing, opening his eyes.

Duke looked at Moses.

"Quick," he advised. "The vapors!"

Moses withdrew a small container from the nightstand, lifted its top and took out a sticky ball of stuff that looked like black bee's wax.

"He'll need at least two, maybe three," diagnosed Duke.

Moses turned the container upside down, emptying six balls onto a clay dish. After setting the container back on the nightstand, he walked to the table, sitting down. Using his fingers, he began working the six balls, rolling and compounding them together.

Jenny had never seen hash before. I'm needed, she thought, drawing close to Ed. "There now," she heartened in a soothing tone, wrapping her arms around him like some morning glory hugging a stalk of tobacco. "Don't worry, your mother is here."

Ed's warm face was resting on Jenny's partly unbuttoned, white, silk gown; on her enormous loose breasts. "M-Mother," he whined, delirious, clinging to Jenny. "Oh Mother," he pleaded, "Don't ever leave me again."

82

"Now, now," assured Jenny, running her fingers through Ed's hair. "Momma's never going leave you."

"All's ready for vaporization," announced Moses. "God's will be done!"

Coming over to Moses, Duke lit a candle and took the dish holding the ball of hash. Walking to the bed, he set the dish next to Ed. Lifting the ball, he held it partially over the candle's flame causing the ball to burn and glow in an amberish flame. "Breathe in," he ordered, setting the ball back into the dish, leaning over it, inhaling the hash's smoke. "Drink the tonic and breathe the vapors," he instructed, taking the hedge apple, shutting his eyes, nostrilling the path-to-dreams smolder.

Moses looked at the ceiling, toward God. "Yea," he decreed. "Oh yea," he exulted, lifting, shaking his Bible. "Consume thy tonic and breathe those vapors," he thundered. "Yea, oh yea," he cried, "Get them vapors down deep inside!"

"Yes-a," erupted Josephine, moving close to the bed, "Breathe-a, breathe-a the vapors!"

"Oh Lord," petitioned Moses, drawing close, inhaling the hash, "Don't let the deep swaller him!"

"Consume the tonic," insisted Duke.

Jenny watched as Duke took a drink and then offered the hedge apple up to Ed's mouth. "Breathe the vapors," she implored, moving Ed's face. Leaning forward in example, she breathed in the vapors, swelling her breasts, doing all a nimble Nightingale could.

"T-Ta-Tonic," stuttered Ed, downing a lifesaving swallow. "V-Vay-Vapors," he said, leaning oh so towards the sweet smoke.

Chapter Twenty Two

Foiled By P.T.

For a while Ed drifted low along the Kentucky Mountains.

His feet were moving and feeling the ground but it was as though he were transfixed in a dream in a magical place transcendent in realm between earth and heaven.

It was miserable hot a top the ridges, particularly in those sandstone places where the trees had decided not to grow. But down below in the deep hollow where Ed was adrift among the moss and giant hemlocks, the earth was soft and the heat vanquished.

It was so queer there in those woods; quiet, still and yes, ethereal.

Nearby there was a small creek full of chub minnows that were as wondrous in their darting as was the water was clear. And all along the path were hanging clusters of late blooming, small pink and white flowers, galaxies of rhododendron; churches for bees and birds.

Every so often the branches of the rhododendron and laurel wedded and leaned over, forming a tunnel of green enchantment that somehow made the mountain paths holy.

As he walked there alone and sometimes stopped he needed no one to tell him about anything. That warbler flittering from poplar to poplar said it all.

85

Ain't no telling where Moses is, dwelled Ed. His heart raced as a cooling breeze began to stir through the dense woods; rain and darkness were talking. I need to get back on top of the mountain to see where I am at, he said, beginning an upward trek.

A half hour later, Ed paused, remembering the tragedy that he and Moses survived five days back; their plan to keep Jenny and Josephine occupied while Duke robbed their room had turned into a nightmare.

P. T. had snuck along, surprising Duke, sending a Derringer ball to his skull.

Ed now tried to quit thinking about Duke, running, catching spider webs and limbs in his face before again pausing.

He scanned the ridge over from him, noting the dark entrance of a small cave.

After having a grouse flush into him, Ed disappeared into his newfound hole, finding it no deeper than he was tall. He turned around and faced its arched entrance as raindrops were starting to hit. Gathering up dry leaves, a bed was made. He shut his eyes, stretching back, establishing himself for the night.

As he lay there with his head half covered in the leaves, he heard noises within the leaves themselves; they reminded him of light rain taps on a shagbark hickory during his best squirrel hunts.

He opened his eyes and raised his right arm, almost touching a fresh-abandoned swallow's nest, camouflaged gray and white and stuck to the ceiling.

Home ain't far; he thought, maybe, tomorrow, cornbread and onions.

Chapter Twenty Three

Encountering Turkey Hunters

Some mile away, camped down low along a creek in the hollow below where Ed was sleeping, two impeccably dressed hunters from the genteel Bluegrass, Mr. John Hunt Morgan and Mr. Lucien Clay Davenport, along with their turkey hunting guide, Huby, were huddled around their campfire.

"Pass the bottle," spoke John's soft voice as the camp smoke drifted into his eyes.

"I flat love this here Lexington whiskey," declared Huby, reaping a monstrous throwback. "We'll get us a big gobbler, come morning," he assured, lifting a fiery stick to his cigar. "I can feel it in my bones."

John sat listening to Huby, feeling the hollow weight of another empty quart handed to him. "Feel it in your bones, do you?" he jeered, "What a fool I am," he acknowledged, "For having hired the likes of you." With his middle finger inside the neck of the bottle, he flipped it into the fire.

Rising up, Huby dueled with his wavering constitution, striving to gain control; he cocked back, wrapping each thumb at the base of his suspenders. "I sure do," he maintained. "My bones do a lot of things. But one thing they don't never do, is lie!"

Gazing at the fire, wondering when the bottle would crack from the heat, John's hand caressed the trim edges of his black Van Dyke. "Huby feels a handsome gobbler intimate in his bones," he confided, addressing the quiet figure that was also sharing his log, Lucien.

Lucien looked at John and then over at Huby.

"Huby," he reasoned, "I find it rather remarkable that your bones, saturated as they are, might feel anything. You've done absolutely nothing since the inception of this hunt but make promises and lather your lard gut with my quite hard to replace, French brandy." Withdrawing two, slender-rolled cigars from his muscle-taut jacket of fine, gray broadcloth and fire-gilt buttons, he awaited Huby's response.

Huby said nothing. His balance capitulated and he toppled backwards into piled wood.

About a half hour passed with Huby remaining sublimely lifeless and then he began to stir. His screechy voice prattled faceless in the womb of rainy darkness. "That big gobbler," he announced, "Will be handsome, alright. It'll have a fine beard, like yours, John Hunt!"

John's blue eyes rose from the coals, slant-peering, checking with Lucien's. Should I shoot Huby or pretend that he does not exist, he contemplated.

Lucien sat quiet as if some mustached frog at the edge of a deep forest pond waiting for Huby to proceed. His blank face was toward the fire; his hands were cupped next to his mouth, guarding his cigar.

"Not only do I feel me a gobbler," continued Huby, "I also feel me a warmun!"

"A woman?" implored John. He leaned back, twisted and lifted a long neck quart from his bedroll, "As in female?"

The rain began to subside.

"Yeah," confessed Huby, "I need me one, terrible bad."

"Any particular ' warmun'? Or would any breathing or non-breathing variety suffice?"

"It don't make me no difference, just so long as she's got red hair. Next to red whiskey, a redheaded warmun is the finest thang there is. I've loved every redheaded warmun I've ever know-d, 'cept Yotanna."

"Yotanna?" asked John. His favorite at The Eagle's Nest owned that name.

Huby watched as John's teeth clamped onto a fresh cork.

After purging himself of a good many saucy expletives, reflective of his dissatisfaction over John having kept the bottle a secret, he crawled on all fours into view. Then, he crawled up onto the log and nudged himself in-between John and Lucien, resting his arms across their shoulders.

John downed a couple of throwbacks before handing the bottle to Lucien. Lucien repeated John's performance before regretfully surrendering the bottle to Huby.

Huby slid his arms off the men, taking the bottle. "We took to drankin' somethin' fierce the other night, ya see, that is, me and Yotanner. And, well, one thang led to another. Before ya know-d it, she took to kissin' me all-ll over. She even tried to kiss me amongst my private divisions. Well, when she tried that, I told her, told her right then and there, to get on her drawers and get the hell out of my place! Why, I'd know-d that warmun fer years. We was once neighbors. I'd even gone to Sunday-prayer with her, once. I thought she was a good Christian and everthang. I'd know-d her fer years, I tell ya, but I'll be dammed, I sure never know-d what she were a quar!"

Chapter Twenty Four

Ed's Explanatory Dream

under the Cliff

Back under the cliff, Ed tossed and stirred in his sleep.

Partially covered in leaves and sometimes curled in a fetal position, he was imprisoned in a nightmare that kept kaleidoscoping in his head, the tragedy that he'd experienced while at the Galt House...

Hello Jenny, I'm Dr. Duke. Come upstairs."

"My redeemer liveth! I hate snakes."

"Sweet bird, the Lord has spoken unto me. Ed needs healing."

"What!"

"Duke is dead!"

"No!"

"Barnum caught Duke in Jenny's room and shot him in the head!"

"No!"

"Get up! Get out of here! We've got to split! Move! Run! Or we're jaill!"

"Go where?"

"Head home! Here, take this three hundred! Stay off the roads! Lay low! I'll meet you as soon as I can!"

Chapter Twenty Five

"Fly Us Outta Hell"

Hidden in a small opening in the back of Ed's overhang, close to his feet in the security of its den, the paragon of turkey hunters, a salt and pepper grizzly colored gray fox, patiently waited.

It sat upon its hind legs with its ears perked remembering the night before when it had rendezvoused with the most game of bearded gobblers.

Now its belly desired another taste of fleshy turkey breast.

The crepuscular creature held still while slightly sweating through its tongue, its white chin, pointed face and dark eyes watched as Ed slept, waiting for him to leave.

The fox flecked its tail and lifted one of its small front paws.

Then hunger nudged it.

Leap-hopping onto Ed's chest, it quickly jumped off of him and spring-landed by a sassafras and then disappeared into dawn's soft woods.

Not knowing why he awoke, Ed rolled onto his side, withdrawing into an embryonic curl. His eyes opened out toward a cool darkness. As he lay there he began to recall, as if he'd just emerged from a chrysalide skin, the nightmare that he had experienced while asleep.

The thought of Duke's death kept him awake and he lay in the leaves ready to emerge, thinking about the queer closeness of dream and life, waiting for the break of day.

A ruffled grouse nearly flew into Ed just as he was jumping in mid-air down out of the woods, down into the cold, calf-deep, silk confines of the hollow's creek; he landed with a miscalculated force, finding that he was snatched tight by the mud. Lurching forward, he grabbed for balance, finding only mountain air. Gaining control, he straightened his back and looked up the small creek.

As if seeing an apparition, he spotted three horses; they were close together; one in the middle was standing opposite of the other two. Near them, around a campfire still hinting of smoke, he noted three men, blanketed humps, and their heads sleeping on saddles.

He strained to be silent while freeing his imbedded feet, leaning backwards and pulling loose, back stepping into water, the ooze miring his boots partially dissolving.

McKay Books & CDs   08/18/14 02:35 PM

Reg: REGISTER3 ID: 4992504

ID	Desc	Price
CB23828183	OS fiction Literatur	.75
CB23593080	OS fiction Science F	7.50
CB23848135	OS fiction General F	1.00
CB23817906	CH HB OTHER HARDBACK	3.50
CB23544789	OS nonfic History Hi	2.00
CI04695439	KENNY G	
	DUOTONES	.30

# of items:	6
Item total:	15.05
- Trade:	.00
Sub Total:	15.05
Tax:	1.39
Grand Total:	16.44
Card:	16.44
Change:	.00

RETURN POLICY
Customers may return
up to 15 items per calendar year.
Returns must be presented
within 30 days of purchase
and must include
McKay barcode or receipt.
Valid driver's license required.
****
NO RETURNS on
T-shirts, posters, or stickers.

Ed had no idea who the men were.

He'd never heard of John Hunt Morgan, the youthful scion of an illustrious family, reared in an atmosphere of wealth, culture and beauty. All that Ed could center on was a black mare; Stride-stepping from one see-sawing, slime-slippery rock to another, he crane-strutted up through the creek, cautious not to leave any signs or dare spook the hobbled horses.

When he reached a spot close to them, he surveyed the safest route to the black mare.

If I can get her without leaving any signs, he figured, they'll think she somehow got away on her own.

To Ed's right was a briar thicket. Straight in front of him, a felled maple tree, half buried in mud, running from the creek's edge perfect to the mare.

Ed kneeled, cutting the hobble. Holding it, he felt the mare's moist breath titillating the back of his neck. Leaning sideways, he tilted his head, staring eye-to-eye with her.

It was mysterious the way that the light passed through her eyes; such queer orbs holding something inside them appearing as if roots or spiders.

The mare raised her head and looked at John Hunt. John has a way with me, she thought. But there is something special about this new person near me.

Ed maintained his balance on the tree while stuffing the hobble in his pants. He laid his left hand down, giving the mare assurance. "Fly us outta hell," he whispered.

Chapter Twenty Six

Comin' Home

The slanting sunrays of late afternoon hit Ed's tired back as he and the black mare formed a lonely figure paused on the crest of a grassy knob close to his home.

Ed looked off to his left through the sycamores and noticed that little had changed since his absence as he caught precious glimpses of the river. Straight below, there was the place he knew so well, a spring fed creek that sometimes surrendered a beautiful red, black and yellow agate that was found no other place but there. He remembered catching crawdads down there. Always having to put his flat hand over them after carefully lifting the rocks they hid under.

On both sides of the creek lay Canepole's cornfield.

Past the field, barely showing itself amongst the cedars was his birth spot, the chestnut cabin; its doorway was open.

Ed's eyes rose from the farm when a pair of passenger pigeons whistled overhead. The birds kept changing leads, moving farther off, going westward along a rise, surrendering, dropping somewhere for roost in the violet haze of the soft mountainous distance.

Lowering his head, he looked back across the cornfield towards home knowing certain that Canepole would love his new mare.

Ed's eyes held tight on the doorway. Riding closer, he shouted, "Hello!"

William appeared and then disappeared.

Ed paused.

There was something queer about being home; it felt as though he'd left just a few seconds ago out the door to fetch an armload of wood.

Home.

Ed knew he was home.

Not because of the woeful silence or because of a haunting gravity that overwhelmingly consumed him.

Home.

Because a certain smell swirled down from heaven.

Mmmm-mmm, cornbread and onions...

Chapter Twenty Seven

Clinging To Floorboards

Ed looked inside the cabin and down toward the fireplace.

He knew every inch of the place with his eyes closed.

Next to the stove remained the only three members of his family in the bleak and dull confines. Close by, batter was turning into hoecakes. Next to the hoecakes an iron skillet sizzling and popping in grease contained fatback, greens and a mess of onions.

Molly was rocking back and forth, smoking her pipe.

Nancy was standing behind her; on her one arm were fresh cat scratches. She was doing her best at trying to cook; a year back, a corn-crib copperhead struck her hand, costing her the permanent use of her thumb.

"Where is everybody?" asked Ed.

Molly kept her head down almost as if she hadn't heard Ed. Then she spoke. "Your daddy is in jail," she divulged. "The girls have gone to take him some food. Your brothers are off fishing."

Will was on the floor, drunk and owning a rotten smile. "I wouldn't care none if Chief Blackfish and his whole bunch come bustin' through the door," he jawed. "I heard your hellos. But there ain't nothing I could do about them or nothing else." Will's head had never been in such a spin; inner buzzards were circling through his bones. He didn't know what was circling what. But he was hanging on, clinging to the floorboards, afraid he was going to be slung off the earth.

"Come morning early," ordered Molly to Nancy, "Fetch some corn into Irvine and get us some meal. Find that sorry thing they call a sheriff."

"Land?"

"Yeah, tell him to tell the Judge, if he wants the Hawkins vote to set Canepole free. Gouging out some slave's eye, and then, Judge Quinn saying, we owe him fifty dollars for it. It's all politics. He knows we never voted for him. Huby never stood a chance in that election."

Molly continued rocking back and forth as though each sway would sprout a dollar or gnaw Canepole out of Irvine's log jail, her eyes gazing off to somewhere along the ceiling.

"Thump!" Ed's bowie knife had taken two perfect spins before hitting, biting deep into the middle of the floor.

Molly quit rocking.

A double-eagled twenty dollar gold coin came from Ed's fingers, flipping through the air, hitting the Bowie's handle and rolled toward the trio. Then, the beautiful coin hit a crack, went under the floor, and disappeared.

Attempting to stand, Will wobbled then wilted.

Ed shook his head in disgust. "Mom," he volunteered, "I'll get Dad out of jail tomorrow. Don't you worry any on the fifty dollars, I'll handle it."

Chapter Twenty Eight

Henceforth and Therefore

The next morning, a scrambled sky full of orange and pink was fading off Ed and Nancy's shoulders as they rode double aboard the black mare along a dirt road sometimes addressed by stone fences, south some six miles toward the complacent mountain-river town of Irvine.

The buildings composing the Appalachian outpost were a square cut stone courthouse that was fine for sunning the blue-tailed lizards; an eight feet square log jail; the sheriff's office with its big window, a stagecoach office near the end of the town next to the bridge that went over the river, a newspaper office owning an editor that swore eating horseradish and raw eggs was best for hangovers, a blacksmith shop and livery that generally harbored a couple of stolen horses, a mercantile store ran by a delicate man that particularly liked fitting young boys for clothes, two brick churches both containing organs that were lifted off the same unattended steamer, some small cabins dwelled in by an array of Irish, Welsh and English folk with histories best left unmentioned, a few brick houses having hog, chicken and dog tracks in the bricks where the animals had run over them when they were being dried out and Quinn's massive saloon and tavern that was now Irvine's official meeting place ever since Judge Quinn had been elected.

Ed and Nancy stopped in front of the Judge's saloon known as "The Wigwam;" Ed read aloud the large proclamation nailed along one wall: "BE IT KNOWN HENCEFORTH NOW THE ONLY LEGAL PLACE, JURISCIDAL

DOETH THROUGHOUT ANY ASPECT OF ESTILL COUNTY AND THE BOUNDARIES THEREOF. WHEREWHENCE A RIGHT FINE WHISKEY, WHAT WILL HELP PRESERVE THE PEOPLE, WILL BE PROVISIONED, HENCEFORTH AND THEREFORE, SOLD ACCORDINGLY, UNDER MY ARTICLES TWO AND TEN, FOR THE PEOPLE, IN GOD WE TRUST, FOR SOMEWHERES AROUND FIFTY CENTS A QUART, ALL OF WHICH WILL GET DONATED TO THE INDIGENT WHEREVER I GO. YOUR HONOR, JUDGE A. W. QUINN."

Ed and Nancy re-mounted the black mare and continued through Irvine. "Why do the cats sleep with you?" teased Ed, pinching down on Nancy's leg to make her squeal.

"They know who owns the best heart."

"They do, do they? Well, maybe. I guess you still won't pick a flower, will ya?"

"Nope, why kill what you love? Hey, where did you get this horse?"

Ed let the mare pause before speaking. "It ain't something I like to brag about," he confessed, "Had to do with a rich dude going under for his last time. I dove off a cliff, swum to the deep bottom, found him, grabbed him by the hair of the head, then toted him to shore and revived his weak but thankful soul."

"I love that story," said Nancy, hugging. "What was the man's name who almost died?"

"Doctor Basil Rathbone Duke; When he came to, he allowed he owed me his life—that's how come my mare. I named her, Jenny, after Virginia. Virginia was the first state in the United States and she's my first real horse. Glorious, ain't she?"

Nancy slid off at the mill and Ed turned around and headed back into Irvine; reaching The Wigwam, he stopped out front, hitching the black mare before going through a set of swinging doors.

Inside, near the middle of the floor there was an elaborate, eagle designed, cast iron stove. Off from it was a staircase leading up to six rooms.

"Ma'am," inquired Ed, entering on into the saloon's spacious, cedar constructed confines. "Can you tell me where Sheriff Land or Judge Quinn might be?"

"What do you want with them?" scoffed a long haired redhead in black leather and a green vest, turned at the bar with a drink in her hand.

Ed smelled rye moonshine as his eyes adjusted.

There on a pool table was some pale figure lying passed out, belly up.

"My father, Canepole Hawkins, is locked up. I'd like to fetch him out,"he explained.

"Get Canepole out!" mocked the redhead. "I doubt you can do that. He's done an awful thing, according to the Judge."

Ed glanced over at the stove with a coffee pot on its top.

"Inside that pot is Judge A.W. Quinn's morning brew: 50-50 chicory and moonshine, hot as hell, black as sin and strong as death," enlightened the redhead, smiling at Ed.

Next to the stove were two empty chairs and a table. One of the chairs had a high back and a pillow in its seat "What's that?" coaxed Ed.

"Do you know Judge A. W. Quinn?"

Ed kept looking around.

Behind a bar made of forty whiskey kegs running close together the full length of one side of the room was an enormous painting of two redheaded mermaids emerging from a river on a moonlit night; their breasts were built up in gobs of oil.

"No," he responded, "I've been gone for two years and don't recall A. W. Quinn."

Ed looked at himself in a large mirror near the mermaid painting, seeing the backside of the redhead having straight hair below her waist.

"Honey," she said, "what you need to know is that he's a HARD man. Do you see that purple and gold thing nailed into that mermaid?"

"Yes," acknowledged Ed, looking at a medal nailed into one of the mermaid's breasts.

"That, good-looking, is one of the rewards General Zachariah Taylor gave A.W. for saving his life during the battle of Boney Vister.

106

Old Zachariah, he upped and killed off last year while dedicating George Washington's monument. Fact is, he got a-hold of the Judge's whiskey during the festivities; Downed too much too fast; too bad. A.W. was going to have him come here and tell us all about the battle."

"Boney Vister?"

"During the fight, some Mexican tried to put a move on Zachariah. A.W. saw what was fixing to happen and throw-d his self right into the devil's bayonet."

"The Battle of Boney Vister, you say?"

"That's the story. Quinn's got a scar to prove it. And old Zachariah, appreciating such bravery, he upped and also gave A.W. saddlebags full of gold and to boot, a white stallion."

"That over there on the table wouldn't be the brave Judge, would it?"

"That's Huby. He's just in from two weeks of turkey hunting, still downhearted over him barely losing in the election. And worser yet, not never seeing nary no turkey. Them the two fellers that brung him in here, if you ask me, they was the turkeys. Talked as fancy as their clothes, they did. After dumping him on the table, they said they never cared if they ever saw the likes of him again. Adding, if there was any more in Estill County kin to him, then God help us. It was hard for me to hold my mouth. I wanted to tell them about Huby being the only survivor of the Alamo and how he lost against A.W. in the election. If Huby had matched A.W. in A.W.'s election whiskey, he might've went on and won. It might've been Huby dealing out justice. But now, look at him. Not no good for nothing nor nobody. You see them eyes hiding below him? They belong to Tom, A.W.'s cat. After that struggle between Canepole and Jupiter, Tom went down to eight lives. It's a wonder he has any. Everybody thought Tom was dead, having a barrel busted on top of him. But a few hours after the fight, Tom's heart took back to beating. That cat has been lying low, biding in the shadows ever since. If you're bound to see the Judge, get a drink, the morning buzz is the best. He'll be here directly."

Ed sat down. "How do you know he'll be here?"

"You want a lie, or the truth?"

"The truth, whatever that is."

"He stops here every morning mainly to see if I'm still around. A.W. loves redheads. He wants to make sure I work off my debt to society. And he's the society. I got caught passing counterfeit. He sentenced me to two years working for him, running this saloon. If there is somebody in here for him to show off to, he'll grab and pinch at me letting them believe that I'm his property. He also comes in here because we've got a spring around back that ain't nothing but that stinking sulfur water. The stuff makes me gag. A.W. says he has to have a drink of it every morning. Allows that it keeps him young and helps him deliberate justice. After that, he checks on his money. If everything is right, he pours his coffee. Sometimes, he'll bring in some milk for Tom. But usually, all he brings in is a hard time."

Ed withdrew five silver dollars from his coat and stacked them on a table. "What's your name?" he asked, watching the redhead pour him a drink.

"Yotanna."

"Yotanna, do you reckon that a feller could buy a beautiful girl's help in freeing his father?"

Yotanna undulated her open hand, stopping it in front of Ed's eyes, waiting until each coin plopped into her palm; No kingfisher had ever undulated in flight so true or smelled the way she did, as though every rose of summer had been squashed up all over her body. "Since I'm the reason Canepole is in jail," she answered with a composed smile, "I'll give the Judge some nudging. But only because it's you, darling."

Ed watched as a roach snuck curious through the door, eased over to the pool table and then went up to Huby's fingertips. One leg at a time the rusty colored bug stepped onto them; the roach then scouted up Huby's hairy arm, pausing near Huby's lips. The insect then got a whiff of Huby's breath and instantly began to backtrack, escaping pell mell out of the door.

"What do you mean, you were the reason?" probed Ed.

"You ain't heard?"

"No."

"The Judge has, well, what use to be, a high-strung slave, straight from the Congo, named Jupiter. And before the fight, was none too tame. Bad sweet on me, he was; Almost as bad as your daddy. Canepole came in here feeling poorly, allowing no man deserved the rotten luck he'd been having. A bear had got one of Molly's kittens and the fish weren't biting. Not even on worms. His sunflowers were all drooped over. Emily, his cow, was clover swollen. The weevils were a-having their way in the corn. Something in the night took and tore the heads of his best laying hens. His own poor neck, where he had

109

that wagon wreck, was causing misery. And sugar, I swear, I can't start to remember what all else. He sat right over in that far corner there, knocking out a quart, allowing if-n he couldn't raise nary no crops, then, he'd raise some hell. He said that nothing was on his side no more. Honey, you never saw a spirit so down. When he laid his head over and took to crying under that straw hat of his'n—the one he says is made from the basket him and his brother got found in when they come floatin' down the river—bless his heart. I felt so sorry for him that I went and sat in his lap and took to rubbing on his poor neck."

"Is that all you rubbed?"

"What do you mean?"

"Go on, what happened?"

"Jupiter came through the front door rolling a barrel of whiskey. Canepole said, ought no slave come through no front door. That did it. The fit broke loose, costing Jupiter his eye. Have you ever seen an eyeball swimming around and looking back up at you from a pool of whiskey?"

Ed looked down at the floor where the keg busted. "I've seen them full of it, but not floating in it."

"CRACK!"

Chapter Twenty Nine

Just a Book

Taking up the doorway, and wiping sweat from his brow stood a short man wearing a dark morning coat and trousers with a white waistcoat and a silk, four-in-hand necktie. His trousers were partially stuffed inside, low heeled, knee high boots. Atop his head was a stovepipe hat. The blubbery creature stared at Ed and then spoke. "Is that your mare outside?"

"Yes sir," replied Ed, watching the man enter, laying a book and a twenty foot coiled bullwhip on the top of a table near the stove

"Is she for sale?" delved the red-faced man, pinching one of his bleeding ear lobes, waddling over to and disappearing behind the bar.

"No," said Ed, listening to the stranger's irregular breathing. "You wouldn't be Mr. Quinn, would you?"

Standing a quart of whiskey on the bar the man labored back out into full view. "Yeah," he coughed, pausing to catch his breath. "I'm the Judge."

Yotanna watched as the Judge squeezed into his chair. "Judge Quinn is the law in these hills," she stated, "If the name Zachariah Taylor means anything, then he's sure to be our next governor."

"Is a whip like that hard to work?" pried Ed, noting its silver filigree and Turk's head butt; it owned a lead-weighted ivory handle and a foot long, fresh blood-stained, sea-grass popper.

"A new whip is like a new woman," remarked the Judge. "You have to break it in before it's worth a damn."

"I imagine a man has to be powerful in order to properly use such a whip," mused Ed, hearing a bottle fall over somewhere behind the bar.

"It's only Tom," informed Yotanna, looking at the cat's gray backside: watching its head motion up and down as it chewed around on something. "That cat ain't been right since the fight," she reported, removing the Judge's hat and planting a kiss on his bald head. Glancing at Ed, she gave him a sly wink.

"Judge, I'd be beholding if you'd let me settle up on my dad's fine. He's Canepole Hawkins. Ever since I've come home, I've had to do all his work. It's killing me."

"Do you see my book?"

Ed gave it a glance.

"That there, in case you don't know, is the number one law book on all Kentucky. Next to the Bible, it's the most importantest book there is. No man is above them two books. And, as the Judge of Estill county, it's my sworn law-abindin' duty to decipher that book, translate it for the common people and render justice proper as it's been accorded herewith unto me."

"What's that book say about dad?"

Yotanna stood up and walked back behind the bar. From where she stood, she could see Jupiter standing vigil outside the door. In his hands was an open quart jar of sulfur water. A watery discharge was running out of his sunken and matted closed eye, and his ravaged back showed rancid weals through the rents in his ragged Lindsey where his shirt was stained and caked with old and fresh blood; brown, red and scarcely dry.

"Let me see, here," investigated the Judge, acting dignified, opening his book to a marked spot holding a folded paper. Taking out the paper, he unfolded and read it, mumbled some cuss words, wadded it, pitching it on the floor. Going back to the book, he spoke. "It says, 'whosoever...shall voluntarily, maliciously and on purpose, pull out an eye while fighting or otherwise...shall be sentenced to undergo confinement of one week in jail...and shall also pay a fine of not less than twenty dollars and not exceeding fifty dollars, one half of which shall be for the use of the territory and one half...to the use of the party grieved.'"

Ed smiled, withdrawing three hundred dollars in counterfeit, straightening and fan-tailing the money in his hand. "Twenty from three hundred leaves two eighty, right?"

"Is that all this means to you, twenty dollars? Did you know that fight ruined my best slave! I had to go on and geld him to settle him down!"

"I'm sorry. Still, twenty dollars is all that the book calls for, isn't it?"

"Boy, that's just a book in which I'm paid to say what's what. That book says a bunch of stuff. But it's me what is the law. And I being the law, see exterminating circumstances on this particular fight.

113

Twenty dollars won't pay for no eye. Not no eye, and a barrel of my whiskey."

"Barrel of whiskey?"

"A barrel of my whiskey got busted up in the fight."

Ed pulled out some bills. "Will sixty dollars take care of your losses?"

Yotanna took the Judge's book, closed it and set it next to his whip. "Sixty dollars seems fair, doesn't it, honey?"

The Judge eyed Ed's money, finished his drink, and took a hit off his cigar, blowing smoke into Yotanna's bright red hair. "There's many principles involved here," he summated, "And I'm a man of principles. What would Estill County be if the county judge allowed any man to do whatever in the hell he pleases? I've studied up on this all I care and my decision is that it's going to take three hundred dollars plus that mare outside. That's my price. And, I'll throw in a gallon of whiskey"

Ed gazed toward the Judge's stern glare, trying to find an advantage in the situation. He smiled some knowing that he was kind of like Daniel in the lion's den as he folded his money, putting it back inside his coat, withdrawing a cigar, savoring its scent as he twisted it under his nose. "Have you ever heard of a kif cigar?" he appealed.

"No."

Ed struck a match along the floor. "They're heaven."

"Are you making fun of religion?"

"No sir. I took to religion on my thirteenth birthday when my uncle Moses, the good Reverend Moses Hawkins, dad's twin brother, a humble missionary for the lost and misdirected, led me out of the

115

wilderness and took me to heaven. More times than one, I've heard the angels sing here on earth. That's how I wound up with my money and mare."

"How was that?"

"A rich sinner from back east with his health all shot to hell, heard my uncle sermonizing about how Matthew give all he had to Jesus. That sermon moved that man so much that he broke down and gave everything he owned, like Matthew, to the good Lord. My uncle allowed, Jesus never needed no fine mare and three hundred cash, but saw that I did. Wasn't that somethin'?"

"The Lord is full of somethin's."

"In the Bible it says he is gracious and full of compassion, slow to anger and of great mercy. It also says that whoever loves money never has money enough. Judge, what guarantee is there that dad will stay out free and clear on this mess?"

"You give me the money and the mare, and I'll give you my word that I'll set Canepole free, and that there'll be no more said on it."

"Can't you do better than that? My mare is a part of me."

"I'll tell you what, give me what I want, and I'll write out a legal statement that would hold up anywhere in Kentucky."

Chapter Thirty

The Best I Can Do

STATE OF KENTUCKY, COUNTY OF ESTILL

30TH DAY OF AUGUST, A.D. 1851

I, THE HONORABLE JUDGE ABRAHAM WILLIS QUINN,
HAVE CAREFULLY REVIEWED THE CASE OF CANEPOLE
VS. JUPITER. AND BE IT KNOWN TO ONE AND ALL,
THAT I HAVE ALSO FOUND CANEPOLE INNOCENT ON
ALL WRONG DOINGS. FURTHERMORE, I HAVE ALSO
FOUND CANEPOLE INNOCENT REGARDING THE
DISAPPEARANCE OF JUPITER'S EYEBALL. I HAVE STUDIED
UP ON THE SITUATION AND FOUND THAT IT WAS ALL
THE AFRICUN'S OWN DOINGS AS TO WHAT CAUSED THE
TROUBLE. AND THAT THE HONORABLE CANEPOLE
ONLY ACTED LIKE ANY GOOD AMERICAN IN PROPERLY
DEFENDING HISSELF. AND GIVING THE AFRICUN WHAT
HE RIGHTLY DESERVED.

"That's the best I can do." promised the Judge. "You and Yotanna can sign on it, as witnesses."

Ed wasn't lying when he said that he sometimes heard angels. They were singing up a storm at this very moment. He sat in the gray stillness, looking at the money. The blend of hemp and tobacco in his kif cigar, coupled with the Judge's corrosive rye, along with Yotanna's winks and apple blossom features, had his stripling spirit adrift on an internal cloud. He was barely fifteen, but resplendent. During his past two years with Moses, he'd learned how to handle himself under the beguiling influences of many an intoxicant, particularly women. "You sign it, too. And the deal is done," he said.

"Boy," imparted the Judge, sticking the cash in his pocket just up from where his gold chain barely advertised itself; a chain connected to a gold watch engraved with a cross. "You're lucky that I'm willing to do this. You caught me in my Christian mood. Get that piece of paper, over there," he instructed, motioning to the paper that he'd earlier taken out of his law book and pitched over in the corner, now remembering what it said. "It might help you."

Yotanna walked over to the bar as Ed got the paper. She blew a smoke ring, watching him read. "What-cha got there that's so interesting?" she pried.

"An advertisement," conveyed Ed, "Beautifully written."

"What's it say?"

"THE GOOD REVEREND MOSES HAWKINS WILL DELIVER AN ADDRESS UPON THE SUBJECT OF TEMPERANCE EVERY NIGHT THIS WEEK AT LULU'S

TANNERY," voiced Ed. He studied the notice a few more moments and then walked over to the Judge. "Where's Lulu's Tannery?" he asked.

"Lulu's is up on the river, towards Beattyville."

"I thought that was Blackwell's place?"

"It once was," informed Yotanna. "That is, well, before Blackwell went off to New Orleans and brought back a French wife--She's the 'Lulu'."

"Think you'll go to Lulu's?" laughed the Judge, grinning from ear to ear.

"I just might."

"Are you going to give up drinking?"

"See-n how I'm now completely busted, I reckon I ain't got any choice on the matter."

The Judge watched as Ed and Yotanna witnessed their names under his. "That's it," he asserted, "Your father is free."

Ed folded the statement, putting it inside his coat. "Judge," he appealed, "I'd appreciate it if you would let dad out first thing when you leave here."

"He'll be in the sunshine in less than an hour," replied the Judge. "Be glad that I confiscated all that food your sisters brought him. Otherwise, he'd've been a hard man to have got out of there for another week."

"Thank you, your Honor," acknowledged Ed, handing the Judge his whip, acting abruptly strange. "I feel dizzy," he claimed, half-fainting over on to the Judge, causing them to fall to the floor. "The Bible says, beverages are dangerous when consumed unwisely."

"You damn fool!" blurted the Judge, pushing Ed off of him. "I ought to have you arrested and thrown in jail! Irvine doesn't need any more drunks than it's already got!"

"Excuse me, Judge," uttered Ed, gaining control. "It's high time me and whiskey depart," he admitted, staggering back to his chair.

The Judge had never seen whiskey hit a feller like that. "Damn fool," he concluded, putting on his hat, getting his whip and book, waddling near to where Jupiter was still doggedly standing under a sun hot enough to melt a diamond. He stepped outside, feasting his eyes on his mare, reaching over for his sulfur water. Putting the jar to his blubbery lips, he held a mouthful in his jaws. "Damn you!" he roared, slinging the jar of water into Jupiter's spiritless face and open wound. "Don't you never hand me no warm water never again! You hear?"

Jupiter's tired head sank down, his one good eye much too afraid to look.

"Damn!" ranted the Judge, waddling toward the mare. "If that ever happens again, I'll stake you out and salt you down!"

Chapter Thirty One

The Judge's Inescapable Nightmares

After releasing Canepole and securing the black mare in his barn, Judge Quinn hid Ed's cash and then ate supper. A few hours later as the chickens around his two-story, brick house stood on their tiptoes and stretched their necks to eye which branch in an apple tree looked best for roosting, he took one last throwback and fell asleep.

For a spell, he lay snoring. Then, a hell he lived every night, his old, inescapable nightmares returned...

Inside a barn. The Judge sees himself as the real boy he once was. The boy's real name is Ralph. He is pouring paint over his retarded brother and while singing hymns. A timid girl, Nancy True, Ralph's younger sister, is also in the barn, making a good-luck, clover necklace. "Nancy," asks Ralph, "Come here. Look down in this barrel." Nancy stands on a bucket, seeing her reflection; Ralph's hands appear above her head. She screams... Ralph grabs her head and pushes her face down... And holds it down until she quits struggling. "Nancy fell in a barrel!" shouts Ralph to his mother. "She' dead! It was an accident!"

The Judge awoke from his dream. Something moist was on his cheek. "What in hell!" he complained, seeing Tom. "Damn!" he shouted, wiping his face, realizing what the cat had done, knocking Tom off the bed. Grabbing his bottle, he stared at the remains of Jupiter's eye lying beside him, looking back.

Forty minutes later the bottle was empty and he was once again locked in another nightmare…

Desert. Rattlesnakes. Eagles. Pronghorns. Jackrabbits. Badger holes. Sagebrush. Bones. Ralph's half-painted sutler's wagon is rutting along, selling a poisonous whiskey to Zach's deserters and Mexicans alike.

"I'll trade you this medal for a bottle," begs shaking hands.

"Where did you come onto something like that?" inquires Ralph, leaning down from his wagon, taking the medal.

"I found it attached to the coat of a fresh-killed hero down Boney Vister way. On some fool carrying the flag."

A starved Mexican woman and her daughter are fleeing for their lives; their loved ones have been murdered. Ralph stops, offering them "Christian assistance."

Twilight.

Coyotes howl. An owl swoops. The sand loses warmth. Ralph asks the Mexican girl to gather wood.

The Mexican woman screams.

The girl comes running back.

Ralph is raping her mother.

The girl stabs Ralph's back.

Ralph pulls out the knife. Stabs the girl. Cuts her mother's throat. Blood is on Ralph's hands. He struggles to a horse, vanishes into the night.

Ralph falls from his horse. His mount disappears.

Dawn.

Ralph finds a cave, crawls inside. Climbs up and over into a crack. Falls into deep sleep.

Noon.

Ralph awakes, hears voices. Two of Zach's officers are in the cave, emptying blood-stained saddlebags; Gold. Tequila. Drinking. Counting. Dividing. Arguing. Pistols. One man is dead, the other, dying.

Ralph bellies down from his crack; Stabs the dying officer; takes the gold. loads an officer's white stallion. Flees to Kentucky with gold, scar and medal. Changes his name from Ralph to Abraham Willis Quinn.

Chapter Thirty Two

From Kentucky to the Mississippi River

"What time you got?" wondered Moses; he was dressed in a white suit, gazing down the Mississippi aboard the Anne T.'s hurricane deck, looking below at Yotanna.

Ed opened the gold watch he'd lifted from Judge Quinn. "It's quarter to ten," he noted.

"Odds are, the Judge stole that off some preacher."

"Reckon?"

"When I first got to Irvine and was nailing up my temperance notice, he appeared, wanting to know what I was doing. I attested, I was performing the Lord's work."

"What did he say on that?"

"That he was the Lord in Estill County, and required no assistance."

"You should-a spoke up for Jesus."

"Son, there's times when Jesus can speak for himself."

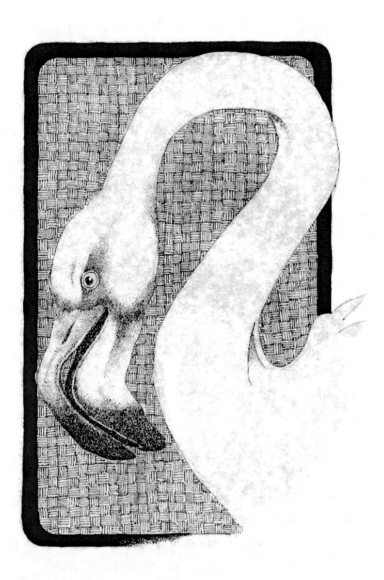

Chapter Thirty Three

You Go To My Heart

"Three more days," related Ed, speculating about their destination.

Moses leaned against Ed's shoulder, absorbing the broad expanse of the river, intent on a log.

"New Orleans," sighed Ed, looking past his steamer's crowned smokestacks, beyond the raised landing ramps. Far down the river, another steamer, the VIRGIN MAY, was stopped and taking on wood.

"No king can match the mellow contentment I'm feeling," praised Moses.

A green-legged, white beaked, black coot in heavy molt squawked and skidded on the brown water. But for Ed and Moses it was just another ballet flamingo with scarlet stockings and ruby lips. The gentle breeze that was kissing their faces and the magical manner in which the scenes were rising and dissolving had a delicate way of transforming coots into pink flamingos.

All that and a sufficient amount of bourbon had transformed every bird, including sparrows, into pink flamingos.

It was a blue September morning as Ed and Moses' steamer swept along north of Ship Island, about a hundred miles below Memphis, traveling on a half head of steam; they were sitting partially inside of a busted bale of cotton. Above their heads, a black, triangular banner flew proud at the jack staff. In raised, gold lettering, the name, ANNE T. undulated beneath the cream of a southern cloud as a bell signaled they were low on wood.

Chapter Thirty Four

The River Inspector and the Fortune Teller

Ed viewed Ship Island and the wild panorama of flat forests in the distance. The endless amount of trees appeared as if a field of green roses.

"It will require about an hour to load the bow and both sides of both furnaces in regular piles of wood," informed Moses. Never had he seen slaves, clad in cowls of salt sacks, so hard at demanding work, so full of reason to surrender, yet, singing, dancing and even laughing.

For the past hour the ANNE T. had been traveling on a half head of steam and yet it had been fast enough to catch the VIRGIN MAY. The likelihood of a race seemed certain. It was often custom when two such great steamers rendezvoused at a wooding that a race proceeded from there to some agreed upon landing. The ANNE T. had recently won such a race with her present passengers and crew, having defeated the renowned LESLY PEARL, without Ed or Moses having wagered a cent. "Claude the Clipper," a compulsive gambler, the ANNE T.'s captain, had wagered and won a thousand dollars. The aggravating thought of missing out on such easy money troubled Ed and Moses. All they had between them was $500 in counterfeit; that and the black mare.

All night long, Ed and Moses had been throwingback while performing their new jobs as a River Inspector and a fortune teller. "We love the river too much," explained Moses rationalizing for his and Ed's drunkenness. "She casts a spell on us."

Captain Claude, a reforming drunk, understood.

Billowy steam was rising behind the ANNE T. when she broke loose with her distinctive deafening shrill whistle. Ed turned and watched Claude smile as he worked the whistle a second time from inside his glass pilothouse.

Ship Island was alive with waving arms and hats, greeting the ANNE T. as she drew close. Moses' reverie of the night faded when he took his eyes off Ed to look into the sky.

As he preoccupied himself with the heavens, Ed's own eyes also began to roam, moving from female to female, until meeting a penetrating stare reflecting back up straight at him from one deck below.

Over 500 passengers were mingling on the 303-foot long main deck of the ANNE T. Every kind of person from the Duke of Charlotte and his stylish slave, Honeysuckle Sweet, who were engaged in a butting contest, to the Irishman, Shawn Patrick, and a German, Fritz Lautzenheiser, betting on who could spit tobacco the farthest. The ANNE T. was an ark of joyous faces but all Ed could see were those pale blue eyes belonging to that redhead, Lulu Blackwell.

Chapter Thirty Five

Virtue and the Evils of Bad Whiskey

Lulu had spotted Ed early on, back when they were all boarding in Cairo. "I have difficulty with men," she confessed to him once had him to her room. "My problem, I'm a one man woman. Only, the one man keeps changing, each time for the worse."

Ed had helped bring her luggage aboard after bumping into her. Once in her room he continued listening to her story.

"About a year ago," she contended, "Jay Blackwell came to New Orleans. He had looks, manners and money. But I learned after our marriage, that he was short on producing the human race. That's why I began drinking. He believed that religion could diffuse our difficulty. And when he reported that he was going to get some Mr. Reverend Moses to deliver a sermon on the subject of VIRTUE AND THE EVILS OF BAD WHISKEY, that's when I decided to head home."

Chapter Thirty Six

BLUE MONDAY!

"BLUE MONDAY," warned Moses to Ed when Lulu left the deck. "You're playing with a fire at both ends and our vessel is the stick! Don't you know, it was a jealous woman that caused the first sin! A redheaded, green-eyed, freckled woman named Eve!"

"I never knew that Eve had red hair?"

"She got that hair from eatin' all those red apples! Son, there's a lot you don't know. Otherwise, you wouldn't be flirting with disaster! Eve was the mother of all the living, the only woman ever born without a mother. Her acting impulsively is what got us all in this mess. You don't need to follow her, do ya?"

"What's so wrong with me having two women?"

"Nothing, so long as you understand the beauty of distance. If you allow two women, especially redheaded women, to compete with each other—LOOK OUT! A woman is the most jealous creature on earth when it comes to love. Them sinking a tiny steamer wouldn't be nothing. Once there was this redheaded gal, Helen of Troy; she caused a thousand ships to launch. No more than did she spit than all them ships hit the deep six. Never forget, a heart is the same size as a fist. One that can black your eyes, bloody your nose, bust your lip and leave you lonelier than hell."

Chapter Thirty Seven

Unconfuted Powers

"Mr. Moses!" called Claude, "Go down and make sure we get tied up proper!"

"Yes sir, anything else?"

"Tell the wooder that we want his best oak! Have it piled as high as we can hold!"

"To heaven!"

"Grab all the tar and oil that you can find! If you happen on to my grandma's rocker, grab it, too, anything that will burn!"

"How come?"

"Cause we're gonna race the VIRGIN MAY for all she's worth! And after we defeat her, I'm gonna buy New Orleans!"

"Cap'n, you're singing awful sweet! But don't-cha reckons we ought to first consult with the bones?"

"The bones?"

"Yes sir! I knew a man, made a wager; Gambled on taking a wife, without first checking with the bones; Next day, suicide. Word was the gent shot himself in the heart six times."

"Six times!"

"And nobody knows nothing, 'cept the bones…"

"That's an interesting story, but I don't start to believe a single—"

"IF IT HADN'T BEEN FOR THE BONES, COLUMBUS WOULD-A NEVER DISCOVERED NO AMERICA! CAP'N, WITH ME IS A CHILD POSSESSED WITH UNCONFUTED POWERS! ALLOW THE LAD TO DEMONSTRATE!"

"Really now, enough is enough."

"Ed Hawkins, tell us, should we race the VIRGIN MAY from here to where, Cap'n?"

"Natchez."

"Is the sun in the east or in the west?"

Moses lifted his face. "It ain't much none in neither, Ed. It's direct over our noggins."

Ed reached down his side and untied an Indian pouch with a red agate bead sewn on its side. "One thing," he up fronted, "What's in it for me?"

"It all depends on what your bones say," proposed Moses. "If they bring us a correct forecast, our Cap'n here would be beholding. Sure to let us in on the betting."

Chapter Thirty Eight

On The Hurricane Deck

Ed tossed thirteen pieces of bone and a Jew's harp onto the hurricane deck.

No sooner did the stuff hit than did he begin swaying while balancing on his knees, making faces, waiting for a revelation.

"What are they saying?" probed Moses.

"Sh-h-h," cautioned Ed. "Be still, the bones, they are doing something."

Claude observed as Ed's face drew close to the bones, inspecting their shadows. Ed's hand slithered along the floor, lifting his old Jew's harp. "Thong-g-g," sounded a dull note.

"DID YOU SEE THAT!" clamored Ed.

"See what?" pleaded Claude.

"The shadow, the way that shadow did on the thirteenth bone!"

Claude was perplexed. "I didn't see any—"

"OH YEA!" interrupted Moses. "WHAT DOES SECH STRANGENESS MEAN?"

Ed's eyes crawled over each bone.

He placed the Jew's harp back in his mouth, sounding another note.

He squinted his eyes and spoke in the most ominous of tone. "When the shadow retreats and when the bone stirs, it can mean only one thing—"

"What?" insisted Moses.

"That there's a storm in the sea of glass."

"OH NO!"

"In the sea of what?" decried Claude.

"REVELATIONS!" thundered Moses. "IT'S ALL IN THE BIBLE!"

"Let the VIRGIN MAY be!" warned Ed. "A dark storm on the sea of glass can mean a bunch of things, but always, it means something nefarious bad!"

"He's right," assured Moses. "I've never known nothing no good no way to come with no dark storm."

Claude was no genius, nor was he a fool. "If a dark storm, say a terrible storm of cataclysmic proportions, was to hit and annihilate that town of Irvine that you keep mentioning, would you change your minds about dark storms?"

"Just the thought of such a storm has lifted me," conceded Moses. "You're right. A dark storm could be divine."

Chapter Thirty Nine

Against His Religion

"URR-UR-UR-URRR!" crowed the pompous gamecock, Sampson, from his brass roost to the left of the ANNE T.'s steering wheel. "URR UR-UR-URRR!" he boasted, arching his golden neck.

Claude stepped from his pilothouse. "Ed," he questioned, would you like to meet the VIRGIN MAY's captain?"

Claude was holding Sampson under his arm, caressing the rooster's head; the cock was charmed, half asleep. "Captain Lance owns nine steamers. For every steamer, he's had a rich wife."

"You mean, that captain marries and divorces for money?"

"I never said anything about divorces. He only marries. Divorces are against his religion."

139

Claude and Ed entered his pilothouse, placing hemp seed in Sampson's brass tray.

"That'll relax my gladiator," whispered Moses, setting Sampson down, watching him peck, careful not to disturb the bird. "I've fought great cocks," he bragged, "But never a warrior with his spirit." Sampson arched his head back, ending his meal with a drink of garlic water. "He once killed a fifty-three inch swamp moccasin. That snake got in this pilothouse and his cotton jaws might have had me for supper if it hadn't been for him. That viper struck forty times. And Sampson, being the smart bird that he is, danced all around making light of the situation until that snake tuckered out. That's when Sampson made his move."

Chapter Forty

The Floatin' Chicken Coop Verses the Bucket

LAADEES!" thundered Moses' voice. "THERE AIN'T NO NEED TO BE AFEARED OF DEATH'S FANGURS NARY NO MORE!"

Moses emerged.

His arms were high and he was moving toward Yotanna and Lulu. "RIVER INSPECTOR, MOSES HAWKINS, IS NOW AT YOUR SIDE!"

Moses slid in between and interlocked arms with both redheads. "THERE AIN'T NO WHALE NOR NARY NO SHARK ON THIS RIVER FOOL IGNORANT ENOUGH TO DARE WANT AND HARM YOU TWO DAMSELS! NOT SO LONG AS THEM RASCALS KNOW THAT I'M INSPECTING THE RIVER!"

"Whales?" appealed Lulu.

"Sharks?" questioned Yotanna.

Moses proceeded to lead the women toward Claude and Ed. "The nefarious green-eyed whale and the boldacious buffalo shark," he expounded, drawing nearer to the men. "Both roam this river in search for inexperienced steamers, and such. Them devils is supposed to be kept a secret among us inspectors. Why, if every day common folk knew what dangers were stirring in this murk, there wouldn't be nary no soul what would nerve up to want and ride anywhere on this river. And particularly if they knew about them things and how they sometimes like to travel in twos."

Ed adored Moses; there he was: a bottle of bourbon in each hand and a redhead under each arm.

"Years back," persisted Moses, "No steamer ever dared this river. There were whales on top of whales and sharks even thicker."

"Are you sure?" examined Yotanna.

"Oh-h yes ma'am," assured Moses. "And that's when The Steamer Association come a-beggin' awful to me."

"What?"

"I rounded me up a bunch of Irvine boys and led a whale and shark exterminatin' expedition. We valiantly struggled for years until only a few smart ones remained. The Steamer Association handsomely rewarded us, naming me, The Admiral Inspector of All the Mississippi."

"Did I," enjoined Ed, moving close to the trio, "Ever mention the time when I was swallowed whole by one of those green-eyed whales?"

Moses turned around and angled his arms, passing both women onto Ed.

"No," offered Yotanna, as Ed led her and Lulu back up the steps to the hurricane deck.

"Ed," yelled Moses, "Are you going with me?"

"Not today, Admiral Inspector. These ladies are begging to hear all about how I nearly sacrificed my own life while saving a little baby; a sweet and dear thing, she was before she crawled off overboard."

"Moses," called Claude, watching Ed and the ladies move up the steps, "Did you talk to the wooder?"

"Sure did. And I took the sugar-cured liberty of charging the ANNE T. with four, two year old hams he had for sale, eighty pounders. They'll slice nice on our victory celebration."

"Moses," boasted Claude, watching a small group of large slaves wedging through the crowd toward him, "You're one damn fine river inspector!"

"CAPTAIN CLAUDE!" shouted Captain Lance, a black hired, brown eyed, wiry figure wearing a Paris green velvet suit and a wide-brimmed straw hat. "Are you still running dry?" he mocked, reaching into this coat, withdrawing a pint bottle and stepping forward from his ebony guard.

"Dry? Yeah. And I'm also running fast. Faster, I'd wager, than the bucket, VIRGIN MAY."

Lance bit the cork of his bottle, spit it into the river, downed half the bottle's contents, stopped, and then smiled.

"Looks to me," appraised Moses, weaving his head in critical review of the VIRGIN MAY, "That thing you're calling a steamer is in BAD need of repairs. It would be easy to understand if you lacked the courage to race us!"

"Mister," educated Lance, poised for another drink, "I've been up and down this river more times than any man. I don't know anything what doesn't wear down in the end. But if there's a blind fool that thinks the VIRGIN MAY can't whoop a floating chicken coop--I'll have to take his money."

Claude and Moses saw how Lance's patent-leather boots glistened and his diamond breastpin sparkled. He was not a man accustomed to losing. And judging the dark forces that stood balmy complacent behind him, he was also no person to slipshuck.

"A FLOATIN' CHICKEN COOP!" rebuked Claude, causing him to half smile, wiping sweat below the rim of his bald head, "I'LL GLADLY WAGER ANY AMOUNT YOU CAN AFFORD, THAT MY 'COOP' CAN OUT COCK-A-DOODLE-DO YOUR VIRGIN MAY FROM HERE TO NATCHEZ!"

Lance throwdback. He stood silent, watching as Claude withdrew a lacy handkerchief and acted as though it was his only concern.

"My boat against yours," challenged Lance. "The winner takes ownership in New Orleans."

"Cap'n Lance," butted in Moses, "I can see that you are a charitable soul, anxious to give your boat away, and all. And I'd like to help you in your generosity and bet you a thousand dollars. A little side bet. That is, if you can afford it."

Lance took one more drink and then threw his bottle into the river. "The ANNE T. and your thousand, then," he concluded.

144

Chapter Forty One

The Grand Steamer Race Begins

To start the steamboat race it was agreed that the VIRGIN MAY would fire her cannon. Lance took pride in its accuracy and grabbed advantage of the moment ordering it aimed at a particular oak some hundred yards away on shore.

When the cannon's discharge smashed into the oak's trunk, it sent the tree crashing into the woods dispersing a congregation of Baptists joined together to rid the world of evil.

Ever since the VIRGIN MAY had been taking on wood, her passengers had been hearing incessant hymn singing. Lance never knew that at the moment his cannon fired that the Baptists were actually in prayer over him and Claude and all the sinners on their two vessels of wickedness…

"Did-ja gets any of 'em?" yelled a voice of hope from some deck below.

Lance took a throwback.

He stood on his deck observing as the fatter and older of the Baptist congregation crawled out from under the tree throwing down their Bibles and scrambling into the woods. "Don't know," he answered downward with a grin, "But if that bunch didn't have any religion, they've got it now!"

145

After the clanging of both steamers' bells ended and before encountering the first bend there was a twelve mile stretch. When the boats got to that bend not a hair on a mosquito separated the lead; At that point, Claude, holding the outside position, executed a malicious maneuver at the critical moment, cutting diagonally across the VIRGIN MAY's path, stealing the lead.

Lance was all but forced into running ashore.

Any other captain would've crashed.

But he got off a quick order to drop anchor, saving his steamer in the nick of time. The ANNE T.'s paddlewheel threw water in the air; the mist dampening his face. He smiled at the insult, soon raising his anchor and eventually catching back up, staying close on the ANNE T.'s wake.

Chapter Forty Two

Situation in Peril

Day turned to night as the race pushed through an awful fog.
The ANNE T.'s boilers were sporadically burning bales of hemp
strategically hoping to rearrange the VIRGIN MAY's disposition.

When the rays of the next morning's sun dispersed the humid mist
from the river's surface the VIRGIN MAY's scapepipes was breathing
sonorous sounds in accompaniment with Lance's trumpeting; He
had become dog drunk during the night, having taken dicey risks,
now rewarding him with the lead; When it became light enough to
distinguish images, his eyes were the same shade as his bourbon. He
lowered his trumpet and looked back at the ANNE T.'s smoke rising at
a distant bend.

Throughout the day, the river's trees, laden in pendant moss, stood
solemn as the ANNE T. gained on the VIRGIN MAY. Claude, now
behind, was burning and dumping cargo around every bend--forty
crates of Bibles being the first items ordered to the furnace.

By late afternoon, the sky was aflame in an opalescent pink; it was
as though a busted up river pearl was spread across the heavens. With
only three miles left in the running both steamers were now evenly
side-by-side.

The river's course had turned from its southward flow running straight west toward the setting sun as the steamers entered into the last stretch before Natchez. At the end of the long stretch, about one hundred yards before the city, there was a bend bearing to the left that Lance, whom now owned the inside position, had been holding paramount in his mind

"GIVE HER ALL HELL!" commanded Claude, hoping to repeat that same brazen maneuver having rewarded him with the lead soon after the race had begun.

Moses was out of breath, having run up from the boiler room. "PUT CHOR NOSE IN THE AIR!" he insisted.

Claude sniffed. Something desirable was coming from the smokestacks; a pungent smell causing his tongue to nearly jump out and slap his face. "IS THAT COUNTRY HAM I SMELL?" he clamored.

"YES-S-S SIR, CAP-N!" cried Moses. "AND DO YOU SUPPOSE FOR ONE SECOND I'D-A PITCHED THEM HAMS IN THE BOILER IF-N OUR SITUATION WASN'T IN PERIL!"

Claude, a native of eastern Kentucky, appreciated Moses' supreme sacrifice and greasy enterprise. Still, it wasn't enough. "GET THAT FANCY SHIRT OFF YOUR BACK AND GET DOWN THERE IN THE BOILER ROOM AND HELP MY SLAVES! TELL 'EM, IF WE WIN, I'LL GIVE THEM THEIR FREEDOM!"

As the steamers headed into the last bend, they remained even, ravaging through the muddy water. Then, the ANNE T. endeavored to shoot over from her position and cut across the bow of the VIRGIN MAY.

Lance was ready.

He found more steam and swayed into the ANNE T.'s path, leaving her no choice but to ram the bank and become entangled in the trees.

A thousand unrefined oaths responded to his maneuver, but he heard nothing; he was playing his horn and touching his lips to bourbon, ordering a victory salutation fire from his cannon. After it thundered, there was nothing but silence; locusts hushed; the black of the night captured the pink of the evening.

Lance gazed upwards towards Natchez.

Down below the city along the river was the wicked part of Natchez, a floating city called, "Under-the Hill." Lance observed gaily dressed, sylph-like forms whirling in lantern-glow waltz; Kentucky boatmen fired musket salutes and Faro players and roulette spinners paused in silent reverence as he broke loose with a trumpet solo in a melody that floated over the water and through the darkness in the most haunting of spirit; Tears popped out of hardened faces; Whores of every rank stood blank, frozen in ostentatious reverie.

Chapter Forty Three

She with Slippery Mouth

"How are we going to pay Lance?" beseeched Ed. "All we have is five hundred dollars. And it's counterfeit. How can we generate another five hundred by the time we hit New Orleans? Those men he's got watching, they'll kill us if try anything."

The moon's silver reflection was lying on the warm water when the ANNE T. came limping into Natchez. Silver was also on the heels of Moses. After coming in to the Levee, he reached Lance's pilothouse noting Lance's arms surrendered along the shoulders of Indian gals; a buffalo robe half covered their nude, lamp-lit forms.

"There's no denying who owns the Mississippi!" admitted Moses, lighting a kif cigar off the one he was smoking, placing it in Lance's mouth. Lighting two more, he gave one each to the two slender, full-as-the-moon breasted Indians. "Here's all the cash I have at present," he lamented, handing it to Lance.

Lance took the money, never inspecting it. "What about my other $500?" he inquired.

"When we hit New Orleans, there's a buyer waiting there, anxious to give me a thousand for my black mare."

Lance quit leaning on the girls, straightened his back, causing the robe to drop. "Do you like women?" he pressed.

"Like 'em? No. Love 'em? Yes sir! When Adam was sleeping God took one of his ribs and made him a woman. He knew a man has to have a woman. Looks to me like you might be short two ribs?"

Lance tilted each of the bottles in his hands and poured champagne over the giggling sisters. "This little dove," he informed, "Is Ho-Wa-Kee-Toe. That's Choctaw for 'She Who Sleeps with the Big Oak.' I call her 'Slowfoot' because she enjoys getting caught."

The girls continued giggling, puffing their cigars, barely understanding good American talk.

"What is the name of this other lass with hair down to her knees?"

"She's Oh-Wa-Ti-Gu—'She with Slippery Mouth.'"

"A man with two such ladies may need a prayer," suggested Moses.

"That's true," spoke Lance. "And any man that ever tries to beat me out of $500 may also need a prayer, on the order of the 23rd Psalm."

Chapter Forty Four

The Voice of God

"This isn't a good time to be alive, is it?" resolved Ed, watching a candle flicker.

About ten hours from New Orleans he and Moses had found refuge among the livestock kept in the ANNE.T's hull; a shadowy place of splinters and stink.

"Just because we have to look death dead in the eye and hold the thought makes it no different from any other time," avowed Moses. "We've got each other--That's more than most."

"Clah-auck," strained a rooster, staggering into Ed and Moses' stall.

"Did you hear that?" whispered Moses.

The poor rooster paused. "Clah-clah-clauck.," it re-sounded.

"A-WOOLF, A-WOOLF!" rumbled a tied blood hound, smelling a cat in the darkness.

"A-NIT-NIT-NIT-NIT!" alarmed a guinea.

"Bah-ah-ah, Bah-ah-ah," wept a lamb in search for its mother.

"GOBBLE-GOBBLE-GOBBLE-GOBBLE!" declared a turkey, daring the rooster to come back.

"Oooo-o-o-o-oo-o-oo," screeched an owl; a mountain canary; its voice was a girl's ghost crying from the grave.

"Coo-coo," soothed a pigeon in the most velvet of tone, feeling the feathered caress of its nest mate.

Moses stood and raised his arms out toward the surrounding darkness. The animals were making all manner of racket; they hadn't been fed in over two days.. "They all hear Him," he beckoned, lowering one arm, reclaiming the bottle.

"Hear who?"

"God!" delivered Moses, throwinback. "They all hear the voice of God!"

The candle flickered, reflecting the wild glint in Moses' bloodshot eyes. Entranced on the rooster, he bent over and lit his cigar.

"Clah-ah-ah," strained the dirty bird indifferent to its surroundings.

"What's God saying?" lamented Ed, watching the rooster and re-claiming the bottle.

For a while an interlude of quiet prevailed.

Then, an unrestrained noise emitting all the way down from the hurricane deck was faintly heard: "URR-UR-UR-URRR!"

Moses and Ed knew that crow belonged to Sampson.

Hearing Sampson, the timid rooster in the stall paused beneath the black mare and leaned forward. Moses was hunkered down, face close with the bird. "Call you what?" he beckoned.

Ed remained silent, touching the bottle to his lips. "It's a miracle the way you understood that rooster."

"Clah-ah-ah," continued the rooster.

"Call you...Call you...U...U...Ulysses?" unveiled Moses, reaching out, reclaiming the bottle.

"Clah-ah-ah."

"Call you Ulysses?"

"Clah-ah-ah."

"Issue a challenge against Sampson?"

"Clah-ah-ah."

"Yes sir, God! We'll do it!"

"Clah-ah-ah."

"For how much, God?"

"Clah-ah-ah."

"A thousand dollars?"

"Clah-ah-ah."

"Yes Sir God! We'll do it!"

"Clah-ah-ah."

"And what, God?"

"Clah-ah-ah."

"Just for safe measure, we should what?"

Chapter Forty Five

Smacking His Lips in Delight

Less than an hour from New Orleans, inside the ANNE T.'s smoke-filled pilothouse, Claude and his slave, a frog-eyed pygmy, Lightning, along with Moses, Ed, Sampson and Ulysses, were ready for a cockfight.

Moses had succeeded in getting Claude and Lightning dog drunk.

And Ed had diverted Claude's attention while he had administered more than a sufficient amount of hemp seed and mole beans down Sampson's throat insuring that the bird would be fuddled and weighted.

Ulysses, prior to Ed's application to Sampson, had been bathed in mink oil and given chili peppers and gun powder creating him into an instinctual and fearful smell of death gone mad.

Claude hadn't touched whiskey in thirteen months. "This water... tastes...rather queer," he claimed, smacking his lips in delight.

"Cap'n, that's because we're downstream from Irvine."

"Maybe, but it seems to own a bite?"

"Drink fast and your bound t' last!"

157

Claude, after consuming several more making-up-for-lost -time, healthy drinks, became one of those delicate individuals who metamorphosed into a bumbling fool. "MORE MISSISSIPPI WATER!" he commanded, half hanging onto his steering wheel, seeing double heads on each rooster.

"Yes sir!" panted Moses; never before had he been so zealous in carrying out a dictate.

"URR-UR-URRR!" roared Sampson as Lightning and Moses struggled to affix the bird's brilliant and deadly sharp spurs.

"Clah-ah-ah!" forewarned Ulysses, feeling Alamo-hearted.

"URR-UR-UR-URRR!" blurted Sampson, taking a step and then flopping awkwardly over onto his face.

"Get up, champ!" urged Lightning. "Come on now!"

"Clah-ah-ah," admonished Ulysses, puffing up his feathers.

"URR-UR-URR!" rasped Sampson in a futile display of defiance; blood was coming from his mouth. Rolling over, he gazed up at Lightning in a helpless expression.

"Oh lord!" wept Lightning, watching as the champ's eye half closed.

He grabbed the bird and with his mouth began blowing into its rear end.

Nothing happened.

Again, the performance was repeated.

Then, Lightning began rubbing the bird's belly and back; Sampson continued to fight for his life but the champ had somehow pierced its lungs with its own spurs; he remained on his side unable to gain his balance, shaking in a spasm and then collapsing into a coma. A few seconds later his feathers flared out and then soon relaxed.

Sampson was dead.

"URR-UR-UR-URRR!" crowed Ulysses, flapping his wings, raising his breast, snatching a horsefly in mid-air, strutting beside Sampson as if he were Santa Anna reviewing the corpse of Davy Crockett.

"He battled until the end," lamented Moses, wiping a tear.

"Here's you the thousand," uttered Claude, settling the wager.

"Cap'n, me and Ed want you to have Ulysses. He doesn't look like much but he's truly special."

Claude looked down the river and then over at Lightning. "Take Sampson and pluck him," he commiserated. "Fry him. He cost me a thousand dollars—but he's not going to cost me supper."

Lightning picked up Sampson by his legs. "What's that?" he examined, noting a couple of mole beans hitting the floor.

Chapter Forty Six

Hell No, Mexicans Speak It

When Moses and Ed hit shore, they cut trail through the swamp never looking back.

After having ridden double on the black mare when she jumped out and off the ANNE T., they were lucky to have escaped with their lives.

"How come no one shot at us?" confronted Ed.

"Do you remember at the last wooding when I sent that meal to Cap'n Lance and his bunch, compliments of the ANNE T.?" answered Moses.

"Yeah?"

"That food was nefariated. Cap'n Lance might know about the Mississippi but people are my speshealitee. When a man's belly smells fried catfish the word, no, disappears. Add corn on the cob, cathead biscuits, molasses and honey and well. Of course there was always that slim chance that one them wasn't hungry so I sent Yotanna and Lulu to them with cobblers and cigars."

Three hours into the swamp with only the clouded moon's light to show the way Moses and Ed felt safe stopping for the night. Building a fire with a flint striker they huddled close and listened to the moans of gators while slapping mosquitoes. At daybreak, they departed from their westward course.

"Thought we were going to Texas or Mexico?"

"Texas and Mexico are fine if you like flat land and bones; me and you are Kentucky. If I drugged you down to Mexico, you'd have to learn Spanish."

"Is Spanish hard?"

"Hell no, Mexicans speak it."

Chapter Forty Seven

The Plucked Truth

Hailing another steamer, Moses and Ed took on new identities
playing the role of a sheriff and his young deputy returning from
New Orleans back to Kentucky with a stolen horse. While on
the steamer, the young and gullible editor of The Dayton Voice
interviewed them, enjoying the zeal in which they relayed their
compelling, fast-told story...

"They were a ruthless gang of outlaws, they were, 'The
Sweeptstakes Company,' that's what that bunch called themselves.
Nothing prospered as long as they nefariated the territory," chattered
Ed to the reporter while he was rubbing and polishing a large knife
back and forth along his pant leg. "That's when the honorable Judge
Abraham Willis Quinn, a wonderful human and hero in the Mexican
war, sent for me, 'Bowie Bob.' Over there is my famous uncle, 'Sheriff
Maddog Miller!'"

"That's absolutely the naked truth!" confirmed Moses. "We
tracked them law violators all the way down the Massassip, down to
New Orleans!"

"That's when we run into them; Killed all thirteen in a fair fight; managed to recapture the Judge's mare, Jenny."

"Thirteen?" petitioned the reporter.

"Yessir!"

"And it was a good thing we never missed a shot as we was low on ammo!"

Chapter Forty Eight

Proportionately Speaking

Returning to Kentucky, Moses and Ed decided to hole up about
50 miles northeast of Irvine at an isolated place on Red River up in
Wolfe County. They paused, staring at an old cabin built right out
on the edge of a cliff. Looking at a spike bull elk skull over the door,
Ed raised his eyes and read a worn sign painted in old English script,
"THE FRIENDLY TAVERN."

"This place isn't much, but it's safe," promised Moses

"Is this a roost for outlaws," inquired Ed.

"Son, just temporarily borrowing somebody's lost horse or
somehow fortunately locating a mislaid ace isn't being an outlaw.
Pernicious perspective, that's what you've got to own the opposite
of. You and I rarely break the law much more than half an hour
on any given day. Proportionately speaking, time-wise, well,
we're almost saints."

Hearing a piano, Moses turned his face toward the encompassing
mountains, adjusting his collar. His consciousness was beguiled by the
late October woods.

It was that one day of the year when the soft brilliance of the mountains peaked and began to fade, when the trees tired of their gold and crimson plumage and began their molt.

"We could have gone to Texas or Mexico," offered Moses, "But that would have made us outlaws. Look at those mountains. Shut your eyes. Let your heart stop and feel their hearts. Can't you hear them breathe? Those mountains and the river are the home we were born to. Those mountains survive in us. Any man who'd up-n-desert a home as elegant as them—he would be an outlaw; a true outlaw. You might think we're outlaws, but we're not. We were born poor river hillbillies and I reckon that's how we'll die."

Ed looked into Moses' blue eyes. Being with him was always being rescued.

"I'LL BE!" blasted a bald headed, six fingered albino owning the chest and demeanor of a bear, seeing Moses and Ed walking through the door. "POUR OUT THE WHISKEY, LIL! THEY'RE WITH PIANO RED, NOW!" Spinning back around the man resumed playing.

Ed and Moses received their drinks from the only other person in the cabin; she stood at the end of the piano; her pumpkin orange hair and jaybird blue eyes took to troubling Ed something awful.

"Do you know a girl named, Yotanna?"

"That's my oldest sister. Do you know her?"

"No. I heard she was the prettiest thing in Kentucky. I thought sure she might be you."

"Last I heard that Judge over in Estill County had her locked up for passing the coin. She forgot the rule: Never pack but one bill."

166

"Ah-h!" expressed Piano Red, throwinback. "If I had a cigar, I'd play us something religious for the Reverend."

"Does this meet your requirements?"

The Albino inspected the cigar, running it under his nose and holding it out before him with a grandiose smile. "Kif?" he asked, hoping.

"Kif."

"What about, 'Sweetly Thar'?"

"Anything, but do please try to hold it down. We wouldn't want any badges detecting our locality."

Red began playing:

"Jesus can make a dying bed

Feel soft as downy pillars are,

While on his breast I lean my head,

And breathe my life out, sweetly thar."

At the end of the song Lil planted a kiss on Piano Red's pink head. "Piano Red fought side-by-side General George Washington at the battle of Saratoga. Did you know that?"

Moses blew a slow smoke ring, poking its center with his cigar. "Yes ma'm, I know about Red and George. If it weren't for Red's brave doings our country would've never got its freedom."

"What happened?" egged Ed.

"General George's top officer, Cap'n Tomcat Jefferson, took to searching high-n-low for a brave man. This was before the battle when the redcoats had me and George tied up in the back of a cave. They took to poking at our gizzards with hot irons and such. They were nefarious."

"I'm sure."

"Cap'n Tom knew they'd lose the battle if me and George weren't there to lend a hand. That's when he volunteered Piano Red. Red had never been much proud, him being an albino and such, but right then and there that changed. Red was the one feller in the regiment Cap'n Tom knew was brave AND could see in the dark. Red took them big hands of his and fetched himself the most awful knife you ever seen. That night, before the battle, Red snuck down into that cave and slit the gizzards out of the whole bunch. Some laid claim they found more than a hundred of them tommies whacked-up-all-to-hell. Me and George never knew how many. It was dark when he got us free and we never had any time to count no dead bodies. We had a battle coming on and we rushed out into the daylight just in time to save our army."

"WELL YOU LYIN' OL' BLOODHOUND!" crashed Piano Red. "YOU KNOW FULL GOOD-N-WELL IT WARN'T NO CAP'N TOM WHAT SENT ME IN THAT CAVE TO SAVE YOU AND GEORGE AND EVENTUALLY WIN OUR COUNTRY'S

REVOLUTION! YOU KNOW FULL GOOD-N-WELL THAT AIN'T THE TRUTH!"

"Oh, then what is?"

"WHY, IT WARN'T CAP'N TOM WHAT SENT ME, IT WERE CAP'N JOHN ADAMS. HE COME TO ME AFTER GENERAL GEORGE'S DADDY COME TO HIM A-BEGGIN-N-A-CRYIN' FOR HIS SON'S DEAR LIFE!"

"I'm sorry. It was Adams. I don't know why but I still keep on getting him mixed with Cap'n Tom."

"You're forgiven," appeased Red.

"Man's nefariousness to man always has him reaching for one thing," addressed Moses.

"What?"

"A drink!"

"There are only three things in this old world," confided Red, "Red whiskey, red skies and redheaded women. They're all one and the same, good times and bad, bad times and good!"

"Amen Brother!" attested Moses, refilling everyone's glasses.

Red raised his glass in salute; the light from the doorway caused his pink eyes to begin blinking. He emptied his glass and spun back around to his red piano. Clasping his bent fingers inside his other hand, he paused to crack each of his scarred knuckles. Doing the same with his other hand, he finished spreading his fingers on the yellow keys. "This next tune is something I made up after the two day battle on 194 North Upper Street. It was a hell-of-a-battle, me and Moses barely survived."

169

Chapter Forty Nine

"We're Saved At Last!"

"WE'RE SAVED AT LAST! GOD HAS DELIVERED ME,
SISTER SALLY, AND THE GOOD RAYVURN REDWORM
FROM THE EVILS OF THE WILDERNESS!"

Ed and Moses paused.

Now, buffalo were rather rare in Kentucky's mountains. Moses, on one pink sunset thought he might've seen one. It was far off over on another ridge, half-hidden against the sky. He was never quite certain that it was a true buffalo. But when Sister Sally came trampling through the Friendly Tavern's door and bellowing her name he sensed that he was seeing his first buffalo, in heat and up close.

"Calm down, honey," consoled Lil, holding a glass of whiskey; she knelt down attempting to revive the man that Sister Sally had dropped to the floor. "What happened?" she inquired.

"Me and the Rayvurn set out from Dayton, Ohio back about a month ago; we hyeer-d God's voice—"

"What was God saying?" disrupted Ed.

"God told me and the Rayvurn that there were sinners all down in Kentucky's hills a-bad-needin' salvation—"

"God sure never stretched the truth on that!" cut in Moses, throwinback.

"AMEN!" boomed Red, flipping his cigar, throwinback.

"Go on," appealed Ed.

"Well, one thang led to another and before I know-d it our canoe flipped and we was grabbed by Satan and sucked downstream. Jesus throw-d me a branch and I made it to shore. But the good Rayvurn, he took a knock to the head and come within a pea of drowning. He were out bad cold. I commenced to gougin' on him and finally, he come to. But a minute later he up and passed out all over again. Satan had us surrounded by cliffs with nary a way out. Then, all of a sudden, I hyeer-d the quarest thang—God's own rich pie-anna a-comin' down right out of the wilderness a-tellin' me which way to go. I commenced to packin-n-a-totin' the Rayvurn and a-follerin' that pie-anna until, well, here I am, saved and in the arms of another man-of-the-cloth and his small flock. Glory Be!"

"S-Sally," muttered the scrawny figure on the floor, Reverend Redworm, drenched and delirious, attempting to rear his head from Lil's calico lap. "Where are we? Is this heaven?"

"I'm not Sally. This hyur is the Friendly Tavern. Over on the piano is the man that showed us the way. That over there with the collar has got to be another Reverend and one of his disciples sitting next to him. Glory be!"

"My disciple is boning up on God's ways," informed Moses.

"That's not red whiskey I see in your hands, is it?" bespoke Reverend Redworm, rising to his feet.

"What? This?" retorted Moses, "Heavens no! It's snakebite medicine."

"He always packs a pint of it in one of his pockets," mentioned Ed.

"In his other pocket," disclosed Red, "He keeps snakes."

Chapter Fifty

Just For Jesus

"Are you all laughing at God?" criticized Reverend Redworm.

"No sir," responded Moses, "I pack snakes to test men's souls. If they haven't sinned, they don't care to handle them. You wouldn't like one, would you?"

"Hold on, brother!" snapped Revered Redworm, nervous, watching as Moses fished around in his pockets. Taking a step backwards, his eyes widened. "Let that snake be! Save its poison for a sinner! Let Satan's serpent send him straight to the hollers of hell!"

"AMEN!" roared Red, spinning back around, he began performing:
"Jes us,

Me and Jesus,

Down on Red River

And my liver

Delivered

A noise

Boys,

Ain't it a shame?

Born minus last names

Red whiskey, red whiskey

Is risky, is risky."

At the end of the song Moses no sooner spun around than did he find Lil in his lap. He wrapped his arms around her and gave her a squeeze.

"I don't care if you haven't got a last name," said Lil. "You're better off without one. You're good hearted and that's enough."

"Blessed is the man unto whom the Lord imputeth no iniquity and in whose spirit there is no guile. Psalms: Chapter 32, Second verse."

"That's beautiful Reverend, you sure know the scripture," bragged Moses. "Have you ever met such a man as you just mentioned?"

Reverend Redworm was fixing to spout something when Sister Sally broke into the conversation. "I have!" she boasted.

"Oh," countered Moses, "Who?"

"Rayvurn Redworm, that's who, there ain't one ounce of wickedness in his bones. Not even in his little finger. All he's ever wanted is to be the Lord's servant."

Moses blew a smoke ring while rolling his eyes over at Ed. "Continue," he deplored.

"About a week before Satan grabbed our canoe we come upon a—"

"INJUN!" interrupted Reverend Redworm, "FULL SHAWNEE; A heathen!"

"Yes," continued Sister Sally.

"POUR OUT THY WRATH UPON THE HEATHEN!" decried Reverend Redworm, "Psalms: Chapter 79, Sixth verse!"

"PLEASE!" plead Moses.

"Yeah!" added Red. "And if there's going to be any pouring out of anything, make it snake juice!" Lil took the hint and proceeded to refill his glass.

"As I was a sayin', The Injun allowed, he were the only survivor of Boone's Massacre and he weren't none interested in no Jesus or none of that stuff—"

"DAN'L BOONE MURDERED OFF HIS WHOLE TRIBE DOWN AT FORT BOONESBOROUGH!" blurted Reverend Redworm.

"WILLYOUFORGOD'SSAKESHUTYOURFACE!" shouted Sister Sally. "These good people want to hear ME tell the story, not you. Now then, as I was a-sayin' once more, we come on this ol' Injun, Chief Blackfish. He told us Dan'l Boone invited his tribe over for Thanksgiving. Dan'l had a man with him when he issued the invite, Rayvurn Jim Estill. Them two allowed, Jesus would provide all the food.

Once Blackfish's bunch sat down to eat, Dan'l and Estill told them to hold off for a minute. Rayvurn Estill explained, how it were Boonesborough's custom to pray on Jesus before eating and that the fort's gates had to be shut and locked during prayer to ward off evilness. Ol' Blackfish allowed, he thought something were queer about the whole thing. He didn't know why his bunch had to bow their heads and shut their eyes, but just to be good fellers, they did it anyways.

Next thing Blackfish know-d, every white man in the fort had aim on him and his tribe. That were the last thing he remembered, except for coming to and knocking dirt off hisself. He found out that Dan'l and his boys dug a trench right outside the fort and throw-d his whole tribe in it. Said, he must-a been the last-n they throw-d in because he wound up on top the heap with just a little dirt pitched in his face. He allowed, that was all the Jesus he'd ever want. About a year after that happened, Blackfish allowed, he run onto another Injun a-sayin' he'd heard rumor that trench was where Chief Blackfish and his tribe tried to tunnel into the fort and murderize the women and children. That a rain come while they was a-tunnelin' and caused the whole thang to cave in and kill ever last one of them. Rayvurn Estill told Jesus had done the whole thang, and if they know-d what were good for themselves, they wouldn't mess around with Boonesborough never no more. Ol' Blackfish allowed, he'd never heard such a lie. He'd been running scared from Jesus ever since. That's when the good Rayvurn Redworm stepped in and changed all that—the Rayvurn learned him good on Jesus.

At first, Rayvurn Redworm told Blackfish how even Jesus' own bunch upped and turned on him, doing him in. Blackfish liked that story. But not so much that he were a-willin' to give his pouch of gold on over to us for Jesus. Blackfish allowed, if Jesus needed his gold, why didn't he come and ask for it hisself. Rayvurn Redworm allowed, we were representatives fer Jesus and know-d what Jesus wanted. But that warn't enough for Blackfish to let go of them nuggets. Blackfish offered a deal a-sayin', if he'd be allowed to snatch the Rayvurn bald headed and knife-out an eagle tattoo on my back, then he'd fork over the gold. It were a hard bargain, but we know-d how bad Jesus needed that gold. How it would help us rid sinners 'n sech. So we give in and let him do it. Besides, we heard there were a bunch more Injuns way on up in the holler, and me and the Rayvurn weren't anxious to rile them none after knowing on that Boonesborough story."

Moses studied hard on Sister Sally's inspirational story finding it almost enchanting. "May we have a looksee at your tattoo?" he derided.

Sister Sally looked at Reverend Redworm, "I guess its ok, but just this one time; Just for Jesus." Proceeding to turn around, Sister Sally struggled while removing her smelly leather blouse owning so many torn fringes.

"SWEETJESUS!" ejaculated Moses. "That's the fanciest eagle I've ever seen!" Moses was sweet lying; He'd seen one identical to it on the back of whore in Natchez.

"I can make it fly!" proclaimed Sister Sally.

"You can?" dared Red. The only eagle he had ever seen flying was the one on the label of a bottle he once consumed. When it soared into the heavens he lay in a corner more dead than alive, passed out to the gills.

"Watch this!" countered Sister Sally, flapping her arms and gyrating her torso in such a manner that made the eagle come to life and be captured in the condemnation of a storm on the sea of fat.

"That's pure Shawnee, alright." testified Moses, "The art work of Chief Blackfish, heavens, how that bird can fly!"

Piano Red and Lil fell from their stool onto the floor. Red curled up into an embryonic position and began moaning. "Oh Lord!" clamored Lil. "What's wrong? Somethin' looks like it's took a hold on him."

"G-gold," stuttered Red, "A lot of gold!" he exclaimed, shaking; his eyes locked into wildness.

"Reverend," fretted Lil, "Albinos is sensitive to gold. Do you have what you got from Chief Blackfish?"

Reverend Redworm reached inside his robe. "It's here, the gold what almost caused me to drown."

"Oh-h!" wailed Red, flopping along the floor as Reverend Redworm lifted his robe, exposing his pouch. "Oh-h, sounded Red in a painful display. Then he stopped shaking. "WHISKEY!" he begged.

"Pour whiskey over the pouch," advised Lil, "It'll drown his pain."

Reverend Redworm went to the bar placing his pouch upon it. Uncorking a bottle, he asked, "How much?"

"All of it!"

"Oh-h," sighed Red; a remarkable change prevailed over him as he steadied himself a drink. "Red skies, red whiskey and redheaded women. What could a man do without them?"

"He's alright, now," surmised Lil. "Put that pouch down in a bucket and pour more whiskey on it. That should do."

"I've never seen gold do that before," apologized Reverend Redworm. "The Lord Jesus never has enough, you know," he asserted. "A little more gold and I could rid the sin in these hills."

"Really?' explored Moses.

"Jesus came to me the other night and spoke about fire fighting fire. He said, if ever the situation represented itself, he wouldn't care none if I gambled with his gold to make it grow."

"Ol' Jesus travels in quar ways," remarked Sister Sally.

"He surely does."

Moses withdrew a deck of cards and a handful of money. "Did Jesus," he explored, "Mention anything regarding cards?"

"Let me see," probed Reverend Redworm, "Yes, there was something about five card stud."

"I wonder what ol' Jesus would say if I wagered a thousand dollars against his bucket of gold; One hand. Red breaks and deals. Winner takes all."

"To wipe out sin, Jesus is a-willin' to do anything!" testified Sister Sally.

Moses smelled 'EVENING IN RAVENNA,' that same putrid perfume he'd whiffed when he'd stepped over that tattooed whore in Natchez.

Sister Sally struggled getting her blouse back on. "JESUSSATAN SATANJESUS!" she screamed, shaking.

"Now what's troubling her?" questioned Lil.

"She's speaking in tongue and scrapping with the spirits," enlightened Red.

"What spirits?" inquired Ed.

"Good and evil, the spirits what move us."

"Make a joyful noise unto God! Psalms: Chapter 66, First verse!" quoted Reverend Redworm.

"JESUSSATAN SATANJESUS!" chanted Sister Sally as she swung her arms through the air.

"Give that woman a drink," volunteered Moses.

Ed stepped toward Sister Sally. She swung her arm, knocking the whiskey out of his hands. "JESUSSATAN SATANJESUS!" she

181

shrieked, hitting the floor in a cartwheel, sending her skirt down over her face and exposing her hindquarters; she landed with a savage force, staggered and then regained balance. "SATANJESUS!" she bellowed, proceeding to repeat her performance. "JESUSSATAN!" she repeated, her boots whirling through the air.

"Get a hold on her!" cried Lil. But it was too late. Sister Sally was in motion, headed for the door; The Alamo's garrison couldn't have stopped her.

"Make haste! Psalms: Chapter 70, First verse!" recited the good Reverend Redworm.

Everyone directed their pleas to Ed. Hearing Sister Sally strain her lungs once again, he bolted out the door and steered Sally to the ground. "SATANJESUS JESUSSATAN!" she ranted as the two struggled along the cliff.

"SATANJESUS!" snorted Sister Sally; her nostrils were half buried in the dirt. Sally and Ed continued wrestling, rolling over and over, captured in the deep ensnarement of drunken and spiritual forces.

"Don't let her up!" hollered Lil. "I'll be there with a rope when I finish my drink!"

Ed roped Sister Sally to the base of a cedar tree; she continued to squirm and rant. He ripped parts of her skirt and gagged her.

When he returned to the cabin he sensed something was bad wrong the moment he entered.

Silence filled the room of downcast faces.

Moses was gone.

In the chair where Moses had been sitting, there was a yellow and blue flame.

"SPONTANEOUS COMBUSTION!" scolded Reverend Redworm, pointing his finger at Ed. "I KNOW WHERE SATAN'S SEAT IS! REVELATION: CHAPTER TWO, THIRTEENTH VERSE!"

"He was sure a good one," offered Red, withdrawing a red handkerchief from his suspendered pants, wiping a tear, blowing his nose, throwinback. "Spontaneous combustion," he allowed. "I'd never seen it. Not till now; Poor Moses, exploded in flames, burned clean up."

"Dear Jesus, try and forgive Reverend Moses," appealed Reverend Redworm, praying loudly and most mournfully. "Lord, I know that thousand dollars he had on him that burned up must have come from sin. But dear Lord, do try and forgive him."

"Heaven's going be a lonelier place for not admitting him," consoled Red, joining in prayer, earnest as a ripe pear.

"We are troubled and perplexed. Second Corinthians: Chapter four, Eighth verse," lamented Reverend Redworm.

"What?" grappled Ed.

"Moses is gone forever," disclosed Red. "From ashes we come from ashes we go."

"None of us shall return again, Proverbs, Chapter two. Nineteenth verse," imparted the Reverend Redworm.

Chapter Fifty One

Winter Wren

Moses said there was a house with many rooms, something in the Bible; the Friendly Tavern had had but one.

He told me that which is of flesh is flesh and that which is of spirit is spirit and that God had created man in his own image. How could that bunch at the tavern all look like God?

The one man in the entire world that Ed loved more than anyone was gone. What remained was his spirit and memories.

It wasn't enough.

Ed eventually gave up his desperate search and fled long into the night.

His destiny with Moses that he had felt so strongly entwined with had disappeared in a strange fire. Death is the only truth in life, he pondered. How could any real and merciful God be so cruel? No person is without sin. Why do we journey so far only to become nothing?

As dawn approached Ed remained saddled on Jenny's back staring downward, wishing the earth would reach up and consume him. Just go on and get it over; a killing frost encased the woods as he withdrew his last cigar in a final farewell.

A red sun began to show-stage throughout the mountainous distance. There in a sweet silhouette was a perched cardinal repeatedly flaring its top knot at its mate which was atop a nearby branch; as intent on each other as the birds were they were cautious of Ed's presence.

As light emerged the smoke from Ed's kif cigar took hold.

In the ghostly stillness as a tear snuck down his face a winter wren emerged from the cavity of an old, slick and silvery beech tree. It flew out to land on Jenny's head, bobbing up and down, glancing at Ed as though they had long been friends.

Ed studied the long-legged, tiny creature.

Something about it was wonderfully secretive.

It was cryptically colored and it owned a dumpy almost rotund body. Its beak was fine pointed and very short. And its wings were rounded.

How can something like that fly, questioned Ed. Why does God create such toys?

Its tail was short and stubby and cocked upright. And its plumage was a dark-reddish brown, with fine dark barring on its wings, tail and flanks. There was a thin, pale line above its eye, and the chin and throat. It hopped into the air and then winged an erratic course through the dense thickets toward the river.

Once there, it paused for a drink.

186

Chapter Fifty Two

Strength from Revulsion

The wren raised its head and tilted its face, reviewing the surrounding cliffs. This quiet place was just as it remembered from the past year. Soon, it thought, I will be in the comfort and safety of my old winter quarters.

The wren hesitated after reaching the entrance of its destination.

From its position, a crack in the hand-laid foundation stones belonging to The Friendly Tavern, it stretched its wee neck and peeked into the darkness.

All seemed safe.

The wren hopped mouse-like downward and landed on something soft, scaring the bird. It rose and flitted about before again re-landing to test the interposing strangeness

Suddenly there was a noise.

"Ohh-h," moaned Moses in the darkness.

The wren's quick wing movements had touched his face rousing him from the rootblack of near death. There was an awful throbbing through Moses' head; his matted hair was caked in dry blood and his clothes reeked with the smell of whale oil; a chink of light partially exposed the charred edges of the boards just above him which happened to be the underside of the floor of The Friendly Tavern. Strength came from somewhere, from revulsion. He raised, leaned forward and looksee-d from the bird's narrow portal recognizing the mountains and where he was at.

Moses then pushed two boards away and poked his head up out of the floor. All that he could see was an empty whiskey bottle and the remains of a burnt chair, nobody was there. He leaned back down, in the dirt beside him was a Bible; Next to it, an empty lantern. Inside of him was a sickness of unspeakable disillusion. I hope Ed is alive, whispered his frightened heart.

Moses emerged into the light to gaze at a grey sky that was rolling and queer, as though the clouds were being chased by wolves.

Chapter Fifty Three

Rotten Ages Left Fer Me

Five days after leaving The Friendly Tavern Ed heard a shot echoing through the mountains.

In the distance he spotted a large bear rear up from its fresh killed elk and began chasing a hunter across a clearing into the woods.

He paused for a while to observe what was going to happen and after silence prevailed he decided to ease Jenny over the mountain and down to the elk. Once there he dismounted to see that it was by far the largest bull elk that he'd ever seen in his life, counting seven tines on each side of its rack.

It took several hours to gut-out, skin and quarter the elk. When at last the work was done Ed left with the hide, hams, shoulders and all else strapped to a tripod that he had fashioned behind Jenny. Leaving, he soon hit a blood trail. "That guy must-a hit that bear," spoke Ed to Jenny, leaning over her neck noticing more blood as he followed a trail which led downward and into a deep hollow.

As they ventured into the woods he found a beaded leather pouch with a small iron pot for melting lead, a ladle to pour the lead, a bullet

mold, two bars of lead, four finished round balls of lead that were bullets, a razor, a pair of scissors, a mirror, paper and pencils and a forged iron flint striker for starting fires. Farther on he discovered a heavy coil of rope. And then, an ornate musket with the initials "KK" inscribed in its cherry wood stock.

A smart piece farther Ed found the bear; it was still warm, lying over a rock, face down, dead in a creek near the mouth of a cave; the creek was running out from the cave which owned an entrance that was grown up in vines making it as imperceptible up close as it was far away.

Ed faced up through the trees; their colors had disappeared and many were bare; Snow was now swirling, coming hard and fast, creating a white and grey haze; big flakes that were fighting each other all the way to earth.

After Jenny was unloaded inside the cave's entrance Ed walked her back outside to drag in the bear. Once again he began skinning and quartering, eventually adding the bear's hide and meat with the elk's. As he washed off his hands in the cave's creek he peered outside seeing that the visibility had worsened and that everything had turned white and that the snow was still falling. "Looks like this is our new home," he confided to Jenny, surrendering to his situation as he looked farther inward into the darkness.

As night approached Ed began to build a fire in the entrance room. Fortunately, someone in the past had been there before and there were several large stacks of cut wood. "Let there be light," he announced to Jenny, repeating the exact words that Moses had often used when performing the same task. When he rose up from the fire he looked along the walls seeing old Indian carvings depicting bear, turkey and deer tracks that seemed to somehow be actually moving in the fire's flicker.

Over on one rock was another carving: "JOHN SWIFT – 1761." Against the wall behind the name stood a whiskey barrel, two red glazed ovoid shaped jugs and three crude, stubby, black glass wine bottles, one of them being broken well in half.

Throughout the bleak night Ed drew close to his fire sipping John Swift's dark and rancio whiskey, terming it, "Swift's Silver." At one point he centered his attention on a log in the middle of the fire that was black and still waiting to burn; around it the other logs glowed in an intense orange color. At times sparks would fly off like spirits and disappear into the darkness. In the flames he beheld the faces of Moses and Duke; gloom consumed him. Why does everyone have to die, he pondered, beguiled and curiously tortured.

There was no honest answer.

The sap of his soul in the form of tears ran down his cheeks and lips giving him a salty taste of reality. Beyond the flames there was only shadow and beyond the shadow, darkness. He pulled out his knife and inched it forward, touch-stabbing a rock; the stage of another flickering shadow. Is that all there is to me, too, he examined.

He breathed in and out and in his solitude and reverie of days gone by it occurred to him that his mother had been in something of a cave all her life having been born blind, and yet somehow she greeted each new day, how could she?

Now all along the cave's entrance there was an eerie glow of bluish color as the moon was full and so close to earth that you could almost touch it; Oddly enough, it appeared to be concentrating its brightness directly down upon the outside of the snow covered entrance; Such a strange window to yet a stranger world, concluded Ed.

The next morning the cedars were snow-drooped to the ground when dawn's light came through the cave's entrance to whisper-open Ed's eyes. He first thought that he was in some kind of nightmare-prison as all along the cave's entrance inside the snow wall from the roof to the floor stood luminescent ice bars of different rank, each having formed during the night.

Ed rose up and kicked one of the bars free and held it in his hands. He bit into the ice tasting its wild and ancient delicacy as he studied a layer of light fog rolling out along the ceiling; mist switching to gelid water; fast forming and collecting and dripping drop by drop, freezing, layering, growing from the top and the bottom, forming the ice prison-like bars.

In the areas where no ice had formed the roof was covered in a brown and green slime that looked that stuff in frog eggs. And in some spots there attached to the slime were frozen cobwebs hanging down offering a strange coruscation.

Ed tunneled through the entrance's snow wall to find that things looked rough outside; the snow was more than waist deep and still hard coming. He re-entered the cave and decided to push his living quarters on back deeper into another room where the floor was sandy; it was a warmer room that was high and full of air, owning brown colonies of clustered bats and possessing both massive stalactites and stalagmites, some of which had grown together to form wondrous columns.

That night the rats stood on their hind quarters growl-arguing as to who should have the meat and hides causing Ed to journey back away from them and back out to the entrance room. He found that Jenny was OK. She had protection and water and some weeds for feed. He put a blanket across her back and then along the low entrance of the cave again ventured out through his tunnel to see an isolated world smothered in white.

He couldn't believe it was still snowing and he went on back farther inside the cave to his rat room and devoted himself to fixing smarter sleeping and storing arrangements; With a great deal of effort he hung the meat from stalactites and in between two columns he looped his rope and rigged a hammock well off the ground, laying his hides hair side up over the intertwined rope for a comfortable rest; all of this he achieved by using a candle that he had made from utilizing the bear fat and broken bottle that he had found; for a wick he used a piece of wood; it was a good candle with a cracking noise emitting from the wick and allowing a low but steady light.

For several days Ed remained alone inside his cave and then one morning he began to hear a noise; it was someone singing, "Rock of Ages." At first the singing was faint but it continued to get stronger and the words to the song, well, owned a rather randomized Appala-chian alteration.

"ROTTEN AGES

LEFT FER ME

TELL ME WHERE

OH WH-IS-KEY!

COULD MY BEERS FORAVUR FLOW,

LA- DEE- DA DA-DADY- DOE.

I AM ME

BUT WHO IS YOU?

I SMELL A DRANK

ER IS IT TWO?"

Chapter Fifty Four

Chewin' the Fat

"Hello in thar! I'm Harry Dean Stanton! When I come into this wonderful world Miss Doc Jenny allowed I was the hairiest baby she avur see-d! That's how come she give me my name! I dropped down from DEAD CEDAR POINT up above hyur when I see-d your smoke a-driftin' up outta the holler! I've been a-havin' a terrible time! Y'don't know whar a por fellar could get a little drank, do ya?"

Ed's eyes lifted to peer out of his cave; there trampling through the heavy snow was a lively figure bundled in red fox hides using a spear for a walking stick; he had what appeared to be three long crow or buzzard feathers hanging down from his hair. Over on one side he had a beaded leather pouch and several steel traps and on his other side was a small axe.

Ed was starved for the sound of another voice besides his own; he had grown tired of embracing the darkness and listening to his thoroughly depressed self, repeating that the only truth in life was death; Up through the brilliant white laden hollow that new voice had suddenly floated healing his loneliness as it had its way with every snowflake, tree branch and bare rock alike.

Once Harry crawled in through the entrance he knocked snow off himself and then stopped to allow his eyes to adjust to the dimness. He looked at Jenny, inspecting her and noting that she could use a good meal; unexpectedly, he possessed an unassuming manner and a gentlemanly demeanor. "Honey," he commented to her while rubbing his hand down her neck, "you're too beautiful to let be starved. About a hundred yards from here there's a level up there plumb full of tall grass, frozen but still good. If your keeper here will go with me we can keep you fed a long time."

Ed watched as the small but rugged figure set down his many traps along with his pouch that was heavy and full of something.

"I lost about everything I had before the snow," divulged Harry. "I shot at a bear and the next thing I know-d he was after me instead of me being after him. Hey, I could sure use a bite. What kind of meat are you cooking on that stick?"

"Bear."

"Bear, huh? Well, I'm one man that loves bear meat. I'd rather eat bear meat than have bear meat eat me."

Harry sat down by the fire warming his hands. Then he reached into his pouch and brought out two rocks, the end of a deer antler and a piece of leather.

"What are you doing," examined Ed.

"Gotta make me some knives for skinnin', and I need another spear point. Doin' it the way the Indians do. You see this round rock here, that's my hammerstone. This other rock is a ball of flint I found in the creek; its green flint, common for these parts. The stuff is hard to

196

work but I can do it. Just takes more time. You can tell when you have good flint by the pitch it'll have."

Ed squatted down and attentively looked-on as Harry put the piece of leather in his hand and began hitting one rock against the other; sharp flakes of flint were being broken off and flying in every direction. Then Harry collected the flakes he wanted and placed them in a small pile beside him. He selected a long, well balanced flake and put it in his left hand owning the leather. Once there he held it firmly in place with his fingers. With his right hand he took the pointy end of the deer antler and carefully began applying pressure to the edge of the flake causing a smaller flake to come off. Again and again he continued doing this each time moving just below where he first started; and each time he would begin the process he would first grind the edge of the flake using another rock; this ground edge he called his "platform." After a short while of determination Harry held up a beautiful green spear point and smiled showing off the whitest teeth Ed had ever seen.

It wasn't any time at all before Ed and those small, twinkling blue eyes of Harry were sitting around the fire, throwinback and chewin' the fat.

"When I was seven my ol' man took to clearin' the land," historized Harry. "But that work went to pot when a tree fell on him. Killed him dead right there. That's when I took and run off. I hooked up with a wagon train. Become a cavy boy. Done whatavur was necessary to survive. I know I'm short. But let me tell you something, there ain't no man bigger than the size of his own heart. I'm Irish. And I'm proud of it. My red hair shows my luck. And I'd rather have luck than all the money in the world. I've been a saddle maker, harness repairer, cook, trapper, mountain man, Injun scout, and once upon a time, the entrusted guide and friend of John C. Fremont. When the Mexican War busted loose me and John fought side by side at THE BATTLE OF SAN PASQUAL."

"You know, my Uncle Moses use to always tell me one story when we were alone like this. Told that story over and over saying it was particularly important for me to listen, had to do with Daniel Boone."

"Good lord, not poor Daniel again. You can't take a step in this state what his name ain't somehow stuck on it."

"The story went that Daniel was off fooling around and got himself captured by Chief Blackfish's bunch. They held him captive for two years. Then one day Daniel heard the Indians planning an attack on his home place down at Fort Boonesborough. That night Daniel knifed a couple of the Shawnee and escaped. In three days he ran barefoot some two hundred miles to make back to the fort. Once there, he told everybody what was fixing to happen. When he checked on Becky, his wife, he saw that she had a newborn--"

"I know, a newborn baby."

"Yep, and Daniel, well, he had been gone for two years. The baby's hair was coal black and its eyes jaybird blue. Kind-a like you."

"I bet that set Daniel's red head bad on fire."

"Nope, Daniel found out the baby belonged to his brother. All Daniel allowed was that he was glad everything had all stayed in the family."

"Why would your uncle think that story was so important?"

"Don't know. But he did."

Chapter Fifty Five

Avurbody Allowed I Favored Him

Just how long them two had holed up inside that cave nobody know-d certain as Swift's Silver and no daylight tore up time. But one thing was sure certain; it had been a terrible smart spell.

Amen.

And double amen.

Simple folk probably wouldn't've begun to have believed how horribly long.

Amen again.

And one of the good things having transpired during the obscure duration was when Ed luckily discovered a barrel of salt further back in the cave; without it all that meat he had would've gone bad.

At one lick so much throwinback ensued that Harry broke down around the fire and commenced to own up to the truth regarding his miserable existence. "My whole life ain't been nothin' but one sorry lie," he confessed, laugh-crying at himself. "I ain't no Harry Dean Stanton. I just made that name up. The truth told, I'm Christopher Kit Carson, the ninth of fourteen children. That musket you have, that's mine. 'KK' stands for Kit Kat. I had a son once but he fell into a kettle of boiling soap and died. His mother, Grass Singing, a full Arapahoe, died of the fever right after. What god-awful happened later on was that I got myself in trouble messin' with Freemont's ol' lady, m-mm, what a little redhead witch she were, prettier than all the red sunrises throw-d together. I don't regret none no way about her and me and what we did. But it's put me to havin' to crisscross this country ever since, Freemont is out to kill me. I never did have me no father. Nope. But thar was this one short, redheaded Rayvurn over there on Pea Ridge in Estill County where my mother use to go to Sunday meetin's, avurbody allowed I favored him. I've always told I were born on December 25th and that's how come I got the 'Chris' in my name. And that I was born in Madison County, near Richmond. That's been my story. But it's all lies. I was actually born in the summer on June 25th smack on top of Barnes

Mountain in Estill County. With the stinking reputation that place has earned, well, if anyone avur know-d the truth on where I had come from, I would-a nayvur got trusted fer nothin', let alone get nary job."

Chapter Fifty Six

A Troubled Neckbone

Drip.

Drop.

What little snow there was on the outer edge of the cave's roof was melting; the white stuff was being fast-anxious to be something else and to head off some place different. The whole thing was messing with Ed's and Kit's spirits. Lord knows, them two had been in that hole the awfullest spell.

"No more meat and no more whiskey and my neckbone is a-troublin' me somethin' awful, tellin' me the weather is a-fixin' to break!" declared Kit.

Ed stepped out of the cave to view that Kit's relayed neckbone message was quite accurate.

Venturing up towards Dead Cedar Point he paused in a stand of poplars; beneath the snow-capped leaves gathered upon the earth, peeped delicate blue and white flowers. Up past the branches in the blue sky so many crows were calling and making war, showing out as to which bird was the bravest while in mid-air they swooped in perilously close at an aggravated red-tail hawk which was quite ready for one of them to make a mistake.

A gray squirrel broke out from two stumps and shot over the mountain leaping gracefully with its bushy tail throw-d in the air; the rascal grabbed a hold of the first tree it came to, ducked outta sight and slid sly around on the backside, holding extra tight to the bark and making sure it could not be seen.

Ed kept climbing, now clinging to an exposed root, at last pulling himself up onto a rocky pinnacle. He had chimneyed up in between some 80 foot tall crack past a dormant hornet's nest to be there. He sat down and looked out across the expanse of forested wilderness feeling the sharp wind. There, close in front of him were two cedars, long dead but too stubborn to disappear. The climb had been well worth the effort. There was a sense of freedom in the air. His thoughts turned to Jenny; she was still OK but she had lost weight; her ribs said it was more than due time to leave.

Dropping back down, Kit was nowhere to be found.

It wasn't until Ed ascended to spend the last night in his hammock that he learned Kit was gone for good, finding a letter in his bed.

Chapter Fifty Seven

"Adios Compadre, Adios!"

Ed stood still by the fire trying to read Kit's letter for the second time, smoke kept getting in his eyes. But the tears coming down across his cheeks had nothing to do with that smoke.

"DEAR ED

AS YOU CAN SEE I AM GONE

I AM TIRED OF LOOKING AT ROCKS

I AM TIRED OF SMELLING ME

I DO NOT KNOW WHERE I AM GOING BEYOND MY
GRAVE

BUT FOR NOW

I AM AIMED FOR NEW ORLEANS

I WILL TRY TO DO WHAT YOU DID NOT

DOWN THERE

AND STAY OUT OF TROUBLE

HA HA

I MIGHT EVEN SEE THE OCEAN

I MIGHT EVEN DRINK SOME OF IT

IT MIGHT MAKE ME TURN BLUE

HA HA

IF I DO NOT GO THERE I WILL GO TO MEXICO

MAYBE SOME PRETTY MEXICAN GAL CAN LEARN ME
SPANISH

HA HA

I AM REAL SORRY I CUT OUT

I SHOULD HAVE SHOOK YOUR HAND

BEFORE GOING

I DID NOT STEAL NOTHING

EXCEPT MY OWN GUN AND STUFF

WHICH YOU STOLE IN THE FIRST PLACE

SO YOU ARE OK THERE

HA HA

YOUR HONOR IS NOW SAFE

AT LEAST WITH ME

Ha Ha

I AIN'T NEVER HAD ME NO REAL OR TRUE FRIEND

LIKE YOU

OR EVER KNOW-D ANYBODY SO HANDSOME AND
SMART

OR COULD OUTDRINK A REDHEAD

I WISH I HAD SOMETHING TO GIVE YOU

BESIDES THIS LETTER

WHICH IS THE LONGEST THING I'VE EVER WROTE

BUT I DO NOT HAVE NOTHING

BE CAREFUL WHEN YOU LEAVE MY FRIEND

THERE AINT NO SUCH THING AS AN HONEST MAN

LIVING

   I KNOW YOU ARE LONLEY

   ME TOO

   EVERYBODY IS

   YOU'LL GET OVER YOUR UNCLE MOSES IN TIME

   JUST KEEP WALKING TOWARDS THE LIGHT

   ED

   TAKE THE ROAD WHERE YOUR HEART IS

   LIFE IS RICH IF YOU FOLLOW IT

   DO NOT BELIEVE NOTHING

   EXCEPT THAT ALL MOTHERS LOVE THEIR BABIES

   INCLUDING YOURS

   GOD MAKES PEOPLE BLIND SO THAT HIS MERCIES

CAN GROW IN

   THAT PERSON

   TRY TO BE A LITTLE GOOD WHEN YOU CAN

AFFORD IT

   DON'T NEVER JOURNEY INTO SHAME UNLESS IT'S

QUICK

   I PUT THE LAST OF THE BEAR ON A STICK FOR YOU

   CHEW ON IT SLOW

   I HOPE WHEN YOU EAT IT THAT YOU WILL THINK ON

ME

   LIKE THEM DECIPLES DONE ON JESUS

   BEFORE HE WAS BUSHWACKED

   ADIOS COMPADRE, ADIOS

   KIT. "

Chapter Fifty Eight

Nothing Smelled So Perfect

Ed didn't know what day it was when he left the cave but it was February 29, 1852. He looked like he was eighteen years old but he wouldn't be sixteen until summer.

As he rode Jenny he noticed so many delicately shaped flowers growing colorfully throughout the woods. Normally they never peeped out through the leaves this early but there they were, some shaped like stars and bells, some like elves' little breeches and some triangular. Ed saw himself a little like those poor flowers being forced to come out and live whether they wanted to or not, only they seemed to be smiling.

And then, something caught his eye.

Slowly, he climbed down off of Jenny and knelt down by a clump of violets. He dug his hands under them through the rich, moist soil and lifted them up to his face; they owned no discernible smell. He then brought the violets up to Jenny. "They're the same kind I use to bring to mom," he said. "She'd hold them and swear nothing in the world smelled so perfect. When I'd try to tell her what color they were, she'd say, 'I know, they're like your eyes.'"

Ed leaned back down replacing the flowers, then re-mounted and continued eastward toward an area of Kentucky called Granny Yeager Mountain; a rocky place full of timber rattlesnakes, scorpions and little else save ol' Granny herself and a fossil or two; Kit had informed him about some possible work there involving the construction of a railroad.

Chapter Fifty Nine

Quieter Than Heaven

Ed had been gone over a day since leaving the cave when he stopped Jenny. Hold here," he said, petting her along her neck as she ate some grass.

He gazed into a pale blue sky evenly filled with scattered small clouds sweeping towards their mountainous destination. Then he looked at the woods beside him.

"I'll be back in a little," he assured Jenny, dismounting. "You need to eat."

Something strange was pulling on him as he walked under large trees in a secluded forest.

It was a sunny-warm day for this time of year; Ed wasn't sure what was making him go afoot; he just knew that he was.

There, in a short while, inside nature's verdant cathedral composed almost entirely of old-soldier-like pines, he continued walking, smelling the trees unique and calming scent. He stopped when he reached a spot where he could no longer see anything but the trunks of trees in every direction; he shut his eyes and relaxed; it was quiet there, maybe more quiet than heaven.

When he opened his eyes he saw one of the pines upon the

ground; its bark was half gone; a tree having died long before falling; the faded, dried mud still in its roots said that it had been there maybe a year; inconspicuous around it were so many cones with their sticky white edges upon each open scale.

All along the forest's floor was a bed of lush green color, some of it clover. And beneath the green there were patches of reddish and brown needles padded thickly underneath. It was somewhat darksome in those woods but the sun somehow was determine to sneak through the branches overhead and down onto the tree creating shadows that moved queerly; some hovered and streamed over its surface as if some strange force ordered them to nervously guard over it; something of a shimmer you sometimes saw on water.

Ed took a few more steps and sat down on the tree; such comfort.

He continued to look at the forest's floor and then found himself lying upon its beguiling gravity, embraced softer still.

Above, the wind was beginning to stir and destroy the silence; the limber tree tops moved and danced in a fancy jig.

"I'm goin'," spoke Ed as he faced the bits of sky. "But one day I'll be back, forever."

Ed walked back to Jenny. "I know you missed me," he confided, approaching her as she nodded at him. "I missed you, too. But don't blame me, blame those pines. They said we should take our time and not rush; Experimentation with honest employment. God help us. Moses would be so ashamed. But we need money."

Chapter Sixty

Granny Yeager Mountain

A few weeks later Ed neared his destination on a Sunday afternoon.

Off up to his right, a hundred yards below a long line of cliffs, he could see the small, well made, stone cabin belonging to the woman everyone called, Granny Yeager; A man Ed met on the trail had described her place and said that Granny was over a hundred years old. And that she hated everything that could be hated, particularly people.

Another hundred yards on down over the mountain there was the miserable work camp that Ed had been searching for; a dirty, littered-up place full of teams and wagons that were hitched everywhere; Scattered about were sheds made out of poles and roofed over with branches; near them, as many slit trenches, axes, shovels, picks and sledge hammers lying about as were so many chains, logs, rails, wedges and spikes; the mules and horses were stomping to ward off the flies. And in the center of the encampment was a large pit surrounded by rows of flat rocks, placed soundly about in a tier arrangement as if some small gladiatorial arena; packed in closely all around the pit were ragged men; drab and dirty, various ages, money waving in hand, standing and sitting, excited and sometimes busting loose with the most saucy of expletives as they concentrated on that all-consuming hole.

Jenny paused on the slope as Ed dismounted to check for any stones in her hooves. As he began to inspect he looked up to note a figure emerge from the cabin and proceed somewhat pell-mell in his direction. As the figure grew close Ed's eyes expanded. There before him, owning a black, six foot staff and wearing a wide-brimmed straw hat over his waist-long, bright red hair was a tall, blue-skinned man; as much purple as he was blue; the same bluish-purple as the violets Ed had picked a few weeks earlier. Following behind the blue man as if every step pained her was a grey-haired woman dressed in black; she owned a horrible frown and her determined demeanor appeared as if she were akin to a wingless buzzard disgusted that she was having to chase down her prey.

"Listen, Reverend Fugate, or whatever you are," exhorted the woman. "I'm Granny Yeager, I know people. You asked for my help and I'm going to tell you something. If you can't smack a rock and make it pour out whiskey then you're wasting your time on those heathens down there. And I mean a lot of whiskey. Not just a quart or two. That Jesus Bible wine-thing, you better learn that little trick before you get near them. When you do, you might have something. And learn to learn to walk on water, too, if you can find any. Short of all that, my advice is to forget the Bible. You're wasting your time and theirs, too. There are no ears down there for that stuff. Nobody wants to hear something about some place way up yonder in the sky where they know they'll never go. Those are cliff apes and they are hard land-locked, now and forever. It's alright your trying to make a living but that gang only knows three things besides busting up rocks and that's drinking, gambling and snakes. You might have the looks to get their attention but you ain't got the act."

"Granny, God sent me here. I must obey his orders. Those men are going to hell. It's my duty to save them. The snake is a symbolic reminder of the fall, an instrument by which man fell into sin. The world before the fall was different: no death, no thorns, no pain, no disease, no difficulty and no struggle for survival. One day the curse will be reversed. There will be no more pain. The wolf will lay down with the lamb and the lion will eat straw like an ox. And the little child will lead them."

"Mr. Fugate, I read that Bible, once. It all but destroyed me from ever reading anything ever again. But I do remember something in there about the snake being the giver of knowledge. Do you believe them men fighting rattlesnakes is making them any smarter?"

"Miss Yeager, I'm afraid that you need help. You need to read the Bible again. When God found out that the serpent deceived Eve, He cursed the snake and commanded him to crawl on his belly forever af-ter. The knowledge that the snake gave was that of deception. If every person was a deceiver what kind of world would this be?"

"The one we're in."

"I feel sorry for you. I'm going down there. And I am going to take this man young man with me. You'll help tell about God, won't you? What did you say your name was?"

"I didn't. I'm just here to find work. You go on by yourself. I'll be along shortly."

"I can see you are a lot smarter than the Reverend, young man. You'll lean one thing as you get older; the best way to see mankind is from a far distance. Let that blue fool get on down there. When you go, find out which rattler they caught under my floor. Bet on it. It was my pet--loves rats—swallow them whole. I wish the damn thing would devour every two legged rat there is. Then I could go back to having some rest."

Chapter Sixty One

Just Like People

"Ma'am, what's all this about snakes?" asked Ed, observing Reverend Fugate as he tripped and fell heading toward the center of activity; slow to pull himself back up onto his cane.

"Down there is the best snake fighters in the world, and all by accident. Six days a week they dynamite and sledge hammer while the mules kick them in the face and the scorpions nest in their sweat rags. But on Sundays, they fight snakes; nothing but rattlers. Tom Whitaker is the fiercest of the bunch, he's caught a sixty-six incher; got him two days ago while the thing was swallowing another rattler. Today's main attraction will be his snake going against Zeke's. Everyone is betting on Tom. Not just because of his snake but mainly because Tom is a sore loser; when the camp first got here a bear made the mistake of invading his tent. Tom laughed as he got that beast in a headlock and broke its neck. If Tom loses, Zeke loses."

"What do you mean accident? How could anybody become a snake fighter by accident?"

"I asked the same question. Maybe Reverend Fugate's Satan drew them in---who knows? What I was told was that little Zeke, he didn't feel like working one day and went over the mountain to go fishing at the head of Hart's Fork. He was holding still studying a nibble when something up behind him made a noise. Next thing he knew, a wad of snakes came rolling down. There were three rattlers in the bunch. They wrapped around each other like nothing he'd ever seen. When it was all over, two of the snakes were dead. He caught the king by holding its head down with his pole and he's been challenging and defeating all comers now for over a month."

Ed looked up; high above circled a buzzard.

Granny Yeager found herself doing the same thing.

"That bird has been following me all my life, spoke Ed, holding fixed on the bird.

"They're white when they are babies," commented Granny. "When they mature they turn black, just like people."

Chapter Sixty Two

The Snake Fight

The men all paused as Ed rode toward them; green flies were landing in their whiskers as heat shimmered off the ground; they were fair
judges of horseflesh, having stolen some of the best, but they had
never seen anything like Jenny; she was a breathing, black diamond
owning a look pronouncing her the queen of all horsedom.

"I'm looking for work," spoke Ed. "I need money and
I'll work hard."

"Son, don't interrupt us" advised Whitaker. "There's plenty of
work. Right now, snakes is our thang. We couldn't race horses in
this hell hole. And we ain't got no dogs nor no roosters to fight,
so this is it."

"Hold on, men. When pharaoh says to you, 'prove yourselves by
working a miracle,' then you shall say to Aaron, 'take your staff and
cast down before pharaoh, that it may become a serpent.'"

"Pharaohs? Preacher, are you fixin' to cast down?"

"No. But I am betting twenty dollars on Granny's snake.
It'll be my rod."

"Against who?

"Against any snake, especially the one found in the garden of evil near the tree of life known as the tempter!"

Whitaker kept a straight face; so did Boss Hatfield, the man over the gang. So did everyone else. Whitaker's rattler was already in the pit and his tail was singing fierce. "Get Granny's," ordered Whitaker. "I'll bet you twenty!"

Nobody had seen Granny's rattler except for the man having caught him, Carl Cain Jones; Granny had took a shine to him because he was quiet and could drink white lightning more than her; he was a skinny feller, up in years. And his hair was that shady color as red heads never turned grey before going white. "Look out, gents, what I've got in this sack, you don't want near!" warned Jones.

Granny's snake fell half coiled into the pit, all eighty inches of his heavy body. He owned yellow eyes with cat-like pupils set smart in a broad, triangular head owning a narrow neck. There were many scales on the crown of his head and in his dark skin you could see V-shaped crossbars with jagged edges that formed a distinct pattern across his back down to his black tail tipped with thirty rattlers and a button.

The two snakes began contemplating each other's moves as they kept flicking their tongues and tasting the air; they raised their bodies waiting for the perfect moment to strike; Whitaker's rattler was a formidable hunter and tried to intimidate his foe, but he was outmatched in every way; Granny's rattler struck hard and fast into the neck, releasing massive venom as he walked his bites and venom along the body of Whitaker's rattler. The two twisted and turned as

Granny's rattler mauled his victim. Death did not come quickly and after a half hour Whitaker's rattler began to roll in a spasm as Granny's rattler began to swallow him headfirst, wriggling as the meal found its way inside his body. It looked like Granny's snake owned the biggest smile you ever saw.

"The Lord's snake has eaten the Pharaoh's once again," announced Reverend Fugate. "When God found out the serpent had deceived Eve, he cursed him and commanded him to crawl on his belly from now on. If all that hadn't happened we could fly like the birds."

"I wish you'd shut up," spoke Whitaker, reluctantly handing over twenty dollars. "And fly back to wherever you sprung from!"

Chapter Sixty Three

Honest Labor

Making the right connections, it wasn't long before Ed got hired at the stipend of a dollar a day, supper and shelter included. His job was to keep pace with two dozen loaned-out convicts, several being the desultory products from Estill County. Ed lugged ties and track and sledgehammered steel until finally he felt his liver shake loose. Or at least that is what he supposed. And at that particular moment as his liver dangled precariously detached on the last of his twenty one days in camp, he announced that he quit.

"QUIT?" mocked Bunt Hatfield's inimical response; he had but one eye, the other having been sacrificed in an ill-fated card game. THERE'S NO QUITTING!" he roared. "NOW GET BACK TO WORK!"

"NO SIR!" issued Ed in a resolute voice, dropping his sledgehammer. "I've worked twenty one days and I want my twenty one dollars!"

Bunt Hatfield issued a malevolent stare. Then, he gazed up at the sky.

Ed and the convicts tilted their sweat-beaded faces.

Nothing was up there.

Not nary a thang.

Lowering their heads they looked back to see Hatfield laughing.

Maybe he's laughing because we looked up at nothing?

Reptiles don't laugh, do they?

Everyone started laughing, too.

It sure felt good.

Suddenly, Bunt Hatfield's bullwhip cracked across Ed's bare back with bloodletting precision. "THAR'S YOR PAY! WOULD-GEE LACK ERR-EE MORE!" he delivered, looking over the cocked hammer of his Harper's Ferry musket. "IF YOU HAVE ANY COM-PLAINTS -- TAKE IT TO JEDGE QUINN! THIS OPERATION IS HIS-N! NOW GIT OFF THIS PROPERTY! IF YA COME BACK WE'LL SHOOT-CHEE ON SIGHT!"

Ed said nothing.

He walked to the wheelbarrow where he'd hitched Jenny, slid across her saddle, gave a nudge and never looked back. If Quinn possessed any memory that was the last person he needed to see. One of the convicts had mentioned Quinn owning a dry goods store several miles down the road.

A sweet, little ride might even the score.

Chapter Sixty Four

Gettin' Even

Shucks, Judge Quinn's store was easy.

No close cabins. No dogs. No guineas.

The door to the place wasn't even locked.

In the candlelight, Ed's blood was up.

The best in man shines when it's darkest.

He found no cash, guns, watches or knives. Instead, there were red oak and willow made chairs, grapevine baskets, lamps, whale oil, candles, flint strikers, buttons, thread, bolts of cloth, pottery, gourds, kegs of nails, various iron buckles, wrought hinges and latches, leather, bridles, bridle bits, chains, rope, saws, axes, hammers, wedges, spikes, lead bars, sugar, salt, pepper, sacks of dried beans and corn, coffee beans, coffee grinders, iron skillets, trivets, kettles, stoves, churns, meal, sides of bacon, hams, eggs, crackers, sorghum, black powder and under one shelf, marbles and a jug of whiskey.

Outside, it was beginning to thunder; the violent sky's lightning illuminated through the cracks inside of the store; the spring peepers had long shut their jaws, diving under and praying for mercy as the woods swayed and sweared.

Perfect, thought Ed.

In a cabin close by, the old indentured couple that managed Judge Quinn's store was sound asleep. They'd finished their evening meal of biscuits and beans and set routine with a load of wood, a cup of warm milk and a kneeling beside the bed with their folded hands in front of their faces in earnest prayer: "Oh Lord, maybe tomorrow that keg of tar will git-chur. And Jesus, can you help Bessie May just a little. I know you are busy but she ain't givin' no milk like she used to. Somethin's wrong and she needs your help. Amen."

Inside the store everything was calm except for a tree branch giving a little rap next to the only window; the pepper and molasses fragrance from the hanging hams grabbed Ed and he grabbed them; the two biggest-uns.

He didn't want to overload Jenny.

But one more load, yes.

Ed couldn't know, but the Norton, Riddell and Hardy brothers, an outlaw gang from Pea Ridge over in Estill County, were also on the prowl having earlier cased the same store. And when they spotted Ed engaged in their own plans they laid low, coiled behind a rock close to where Jenny was tied.

"Hope this ain't too much on you," whispered Ed to Jenny as he struggled to balance two enormous hams across her neck.

"THUMP!"

The world stopped.

Ed had gotten himself cold-cocked, falling unconscious.

The Pea Ridge gang took his coat, boots, Jenny and all he had stolen. Then they went back into the store stealing more. When they were loaded down and ready to leave they looked over at Ed.

"What'll we do with him?" asked one of the Riddells as he sat on Jenny, petting one of the hams.

"Makes me never no mind," answered the oldest Norton, pulling out a knife, considering Ed's throat.

"Leave him," ordered one of the Hardy brothers. "He's dead anyways."

Chapter Sixty Five

Jes Like A Baby

Ed regained full consciousness a day and a half later.

Waking, he had but one thought, Am I in a nightmare?

BARS.

Am I back in the cave?

Shutting his eyes, he dared not open them for the longest time.
When he did, he again saw the bars.

These were not bars made of ice.

On the other side of them stood the content Judge Quinn.

Ed tried to stand, but couldn't.

Chains.

"Err-ya a little weighted down, err-ya?" scoffed Judge Quinn. "Too
bad your partners run off and left you with that bump on your noggin.
Too bad you can't stand. I like for a prisoner to stand when I hand
down my verdict."

Ed moaned while feeling the back of his sore head. "V-verdict," he
stuttered, confused

"Yeah, boy, you slept through your trial jes like a baby."

Ed looked at his bare feet. "Where's my boots?" he asked.

"Don't-chu worry nary none about no boots, that's something the convicts make at our state penitentiary. You'll have two years to make boots. That's my verdict; A year for each ham. I could make it longer, but I like you. One day you might even make me a fair deputy--what do you say to that?"

Ed held stove still, sizing his situation. Anyone could sing a lie in a world mired in illusion. He loathed any yellow cur hiding behind the law. "Judge," he responded. "You captured me fair-n-square. All things considered, getting two years ain't bad. When I get freed, I'll be your deputy."

Chapter Sixty Six

Opus Nefas

Three rough days later, when Ed's hack arrived at the state penitentiary in Frankfort, Kentucky, he was booted out onto the ground; it was a hot noon and the dust from the hack was settling; he was fettered in chains as he spit dirt while managing to rise; Before him, a moat encircled an impregnable stone fortress.

"LOWER THE GATE!" shouted one of Ed's guards, spitting tobacco.

As the drawbridge began to lower, so did Ed's heart.

Down, down it came, hitting the hard ground, jarring his soul.

Upon entering, he collapsed to the ground and began to jerk, moan and speak in tongue.

"Get the warden," ordered one of the blue-suited prison guards.

When the warden arrived, he saw Ed curled up into a ball. "Who is he?" he asked, looking with particular interest.

"The new prisoner, sir," informed a guard, "his name is Edward W. Hawkins. He's a low down ham thief from Estill County. The Judge over there said we had two years to straighten him out."

The warden gave a hard stare down at Ed's trembling figure.

"Sir, what should we do with him?"

"Do? Mister Conrad, have you no mercy? Can't you see? This young man is suffering from opus nefas."

"What?"

"It's a rare and fluctuating nervous disorder. Any stress whatsoever results in a fit, deep sleep, delirium or even death. It grabs a man's backbone, rendering him lame and almost useless. No person who has ever had it has lived longer than two years. This poor man could go at any moment. Look at him. He'll need infinite amounts of rest and special duties directed strictly by me, as well as my tonic and vapors. Mr. Conrad, do you like fish? Of course you do. Mr. Conrad, I need fish and this prison needs fish. We never have fish, do we? We are long overdue for fresh fish straight from the Kentucky River. Remember, Mr. Conrad, a well-fed prisoner is much less apt to devote himself to escape. You know, of course, if we lose a prisoner by death or escape, it looks bad. Such a thing could cost us our jobs. You wouldn't want that, would you? Of course you wouldn't. Now then, I feel that we can easily trust this man...Who did you say he was?"

"Edward W. Hawkins, sir."

"Yes, that was it, Edward W. Hawkins, a rather noble sounding name, isn't it? I'm assigning this Edward W. Hawkins, once he's better, to the sole duty of supplying our prison with however many fish he can catch.

I'll expect you to furnish the poles, line, bait, hooks and knife. I'll personally see to it that he receives the necessary tonic and vapors."

230

Chapter Sixty Seven

A Familiar Voice

That voice, was it Duke's?

Ed kept his eyes locked, afraid his ears were being tricked.

"You guards may leave now," spoke Warden Gray. "It is imperative that this prisoner be left alone during the administration of my tonic and vapors. Opis Nefas, umm-umm, the worst I've ever seen."

Almost a minute of silence passed before Ed heard the strike of a match; then, the odor of kif, that blend of hemp and tobacco.

"Ed, you can get up now, they're gone."

Ed moved his arms and opened his eyes.

Reality?

Before Ed, stood Duke, slick dressed, silver-haired, holding his silver flask and a cigar.

"Hell or heaven makes no difference; it's the ride that counts."

Ed stood up, taking the tonic and vapors; Duke's fingers were stained in ink.

Ed throwdback. Then throwdback again and then spoke. "Are you an angel?"

"What do you believe?"

"I don't know. You seem like one."

"Angels have wings. See any on me?"

Duke's back was wingless. "Barnum murdered you. Nobody can whoop death."

"I did. I sailed through a cool blackness and knew that I was dead."

"As dead as this flask?" asked Ed, holding it upside down, showing that it was empty.

"Deader," declared Duke, returning the empty to his coat, withdrawing another. "But like this flask, I came back. Back once more to be with the living."

"How?"

"I don't know. All I remember before dying was being bent over inspecting Jenny's trunk. I heard a gunshot. Then a force sailed me through oblivion. When I got to heaven, there sat Saint Peter reviewing my history, unfortunately, every detail. I stood in attention about an hour, then he slammed shut his book. 'Mr. Duke,' he said. 'The reports show that you lied to women, cheated at cards, fixed horse races, counterfeited and stole whiskey. But you haven't been so bad that we're going to send you straight to Hell because nobody is perfect. What we've decided is to place you back in Kentucky to give you one more chance.'

Next I knew, raindrops started kissing my face and I was back alive. I opened my eyes. There was a full moon so close I thought I could touch it. I heard some mumbo-jumbo. I sat up. Head level with me, not far off, were two heads going up and down; they were digging away in what was my grave. I was starting to let those diggers know that they needn't labor on when a pain overtook me and I broke loose with a moan. After that, well, I was unable to tell them anything; I never saw such fine runners as I must have frightened them. All in one motion, they knocked over the lantern and vanished. Where they went is any man's guess. I'd venture to say, judging by the rate of their speed, they may well have reached the African interior by dawn of the next day. That is, if they didn't go through Irvine. If they made that mistake, that's as far as they got."

"How did you wind up as the warden?"

"I obtained my wardenship just like any warden does. I lied about who I was and what I was."

"That simple, huh?"

"You see, politicians can't get along without their 'hollow logs.' I had to slip $1,000 cash in our governor's 'hollow log' in order to help him reach the decision that I was the best qualified for wardening."

"Good money?"

"Almost."

Ed breathed a sigh of relief. "How come you wanted to be the warden?"

Duke throwdback, followed by a perfect smoke ring. "I wanted to see old friends. Besides, can you think of a finer place to make counterfeit?"

It's Duke, alright, pondered Ed. The angel has transformed this hell into heaven.

Down in the prison yard Mr. Conrad was explaining about Opus Nefas to his fellow guards and a gang of prisoners. Everyone was agreeing to make Ed's last days easy. Whatever that lad desired, they'd be there for him, that poor feller.

Chapter Sixty Eight

Some Things Come Natural

Late the next afternoon, alone, Ed was situated along a sandy bank down low at a shady spot where a creek fed into the river. No sooner were his poles spread than he started getting a bite. Ed's biggest pole bent and began to pull loose through the forked rest, going out into the river. He grabbed the pole with one hand and with his other he placed a knife in his jaws. Once his teeth were clamped he held strong to the pole as it began to pull him into the green water; foot by foot he stubbornly lost ground until he found himself chest deep. And then, he disappeared, going under…

Chapter Sixty Nine

WAKE THE WARDEN!

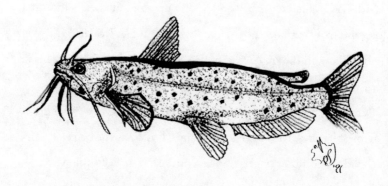

At dawn of the next day, the prison's watchtower's bell began to ring. "WAKE CONRAD!" cried a guard. "TELL HIM TO GET HERE FAST!"

Minutes later, a half uniformed Conrad stood in the tower. "WAKE THE WARDEN!" he shouted to the ground guards.

Duke walked up three flights of steps and then stopped. "RING THE BELL," he ordered. "MR. CONRAD! RING HER LOUD FOR TEN FULL MINUTES! HAVE EVERY MAN ASSEMBLED ALONG THE FRONT WALL! "

"Yessir!" snapped Conrad. "Here's the ten dollars I owe."

"Keep your money. It wasn't a fair bet. I knew any soul suffering from Opus Nefas would never consider escape."

After the bell stopped an almost religious stillness reigned as every grizzled, gruff and greasy face gazed out and gawked down. Then, an anonymous voice burst loose. "THAT AIN'T NO REAL CATFISH, IS IT!"

Ed stood outside the prison looking up at all the heads mounted along the front wall of the prison. "REAL? WHAT'S REAL?" Walking back behind the ox having pulled his catfish, he withdrew his knife from the yellow monster.

"Garl derndess thang I avur see-d," commented the tower guard. "My pappy swore thar were sech thangs, but I nayvur believed him."

"Had a good dog once," spoke Conrad. "The last time we saw him he was swimming the river. We never knew what got him. Now, I know."

"Them whiskers is as long and lean as Yotanna's legs," sighed a voice.

"And twice as slippery," spilled a guard, three heads down the line.

"DO YOU LIKE CATFISH!" yelled Ed up to the men; his wavy black hair was slicked back and his face had matured as though he had somehow aged a year or more in his brief absence from the prison.

Duke throwdback. "CATFISH! CORNBREAD! SOUP BEANS! ONIONS! POLK! AND RED WHISKEY! THAT'S TONIGHT'S DINNER FOR EVERYONE!" he announced.

The tangled mess of mankind erupted in cheer.

"LOWER THE BRIDGE!" boomed Duke. "MAKE WAY FOR THE CATFISH KING!"

Chapter Seventy

A Night to Remember

Nightfall.

The prison yard.

Such a gathering of good will and brotherhood.

A warden's dream.

Thick, white, fried catfish steaks and red whiskey graced ever parched liver.

Midway into the festivity, Ed started ringing the tower bell.

When he stopped, he moved to stand in between two torches beside Duke; behind them lay a smoke-ringed moon.

"GENTLEMAN!" announced Duke down to the crowded tables. "WE'VE GOT THE CATFISH KING! WE'VE GOT CATFISH! WE'VE GOT WHISKEY--"

"AND OUTSIDE OUR WALLS," interrupted Ed, "THANKS TO THE BEST WARDEN STRAIGHT DOWN FROM HEAVEN, WE'VE GOT A WAGON OF WILD, WAITIN' AND WANTIN' WOMEN!"

Duke raised his horn, shaking the stars with successive high notes. "LOWER THE BRIDGE!" he commanded. "TONIGHT IS A NIGHT TO REMEMBER!"

Chapter Seventy One

How America Got Its Freedom

"Honey," spoke Ed when a petite girl came and sat down by him; a demure dark-haired girl owning dark eyes; "What's your name?"

"Dixie."

"Dixie? I wouldn't-ve guessed that. How did-ju get that name?"

"I'm from New Orleans. And I am always on the lookout for a ten dollar bill."

"Ten dollars, huh, and I thought you were shy. If you play your cards right you might get a twenty."

"With you, mm-m, I might not want a cent."

"Did you happen to know, if it weren't for fishing that there wouldn't be any such thing as America?"

"What?"

"Without fishing, darlin', America would never had gotten its freedom."

"Come on now, you're full of it."

"No, it's the truth."

"The truth my eye--The only truth in this world is there are no truths."

"Have you ever heard of George Washington?"

"What about him?"

"Back during the Revolutionary War, he was running the whole show. And there was this one winter where his army was camped down low at a place called, Valley Forge. They say that when he was there it snowed ten feet deep and the river froze over so bad that you could run a team of mules across it."

"What's that got to do with America getting its freedom?"

"If you will allow me to continue, I'll tell you."

"Go on. Looks like I'm stuck."

"You see, Washington had this army that was fighting the redcoats to get America's freedom. The redcoats were the worthless soldiers from England. England was called Great Brittan. But after they met Washington they found out just how great they were. That bunch was over here in our own country ordering us what we could and could not do and Washington was fed up with it. He got up an army to tell the British where they could go. And the British, they didn't like it none too good. My uncle Moses was in that army. And him and his Irvine boys was camped down low with Washington at Valley Forge on that bad winter when Washington come-a-beggin' to him. 'Colonel Moses,' he said, 'do you think you and your brave Irvine boys could go out there on that Delaware River and catch my army some catfish? Y My army's spirits are bad low, and, as you know, there ain't nothin' like a mess of fresh fried catfish that can change a man's outlook on life."

242

"How did they fish if the river was frozen?"

"Simple. They took and got some big, double-bladed axes and chopped through. Once that was done they got in a boat and went out in the middle where they know'd the biggest-uns likely was. They dropped their lines and after a spell they took and heard something over on the other side. What is that, they kept wondering. The more they listened the more it sounded just like a bunch of hogs, a-rootin'-n-a-goin' on. That got them to pull their boat up and sneak over on the other side. If there was one thing better than catfish it was fresh hog meat. Well, when they got there they didn't find no hogs. But they did find something nefarious."

"What?"

"Hessians."

"Hessians?"

"Yep."

"What's Hessians?"

"They was worstest of the worst. Nothing but the devil's disciples hired out by the cowardly redcoats; assassins to kill America. But when my uncle Moses spotted them all there passed out drunk and wrapped tight in their blankets sound asleep and a-snorin' up a storm and a-soundin' like hogs, that's when him and his Irvine boys done 'em in; slit their gizzards and dulled a dozen good knives in the process. So, you see, if it hadn't been for my uncle going fishin' there wouldn'tve never been no America. Most likely, them Hessians would-a snuck up on us instead the other way around."

Chapter Seventy Two

More Than You Know

For two years things went peachy; it was a prison of ridiculousness, just like any prison, but with far more sunshine. Then came the awful day when Ed actually had to leave; his debt having been paid to society and then some.

"I reckon this is good-bye," spoke Ed, handing Duke his flask.

"Keep it," insisted Duke. "If you ever go back to Estill County, you'll need it."

For a spell, a stretch of silence prevailed; both men knew that this would be the last time they would ever see each other.

And home was whispering out to Ed.

Duke shook his head. "Spontaneous combustion," he lamented. "We all know we have to go, but to where?"

"You miss him too, don't you?"

"More than you know."

"We'll never see him again."

"If Doc Davenport is right, you may be wrong. I might join him any day."

"What do you mean?"

"Ever since being shot I've been having blackouts. At first they weren't bad. But lately, well, they've gotten worse, a lot worse. Doc says my next blackout may be my last. At best, he's giving me a couple of months."

"How can he be so sure?"

"He was an army doctor before he came here; saw a lot of head wounds that took their sweet time."

"Why didn't you tell me before?"

"When you first got here, the blackouts weren't too bad. A few months ago, when I went to the Doc, well, I saw no reason in burdening you. I gave strict orders to Conrad to tell no one."

"Why are you telling me now?"

"I don't want you on the outside thinking it will be rosy if you get in trouble again."

"I'd like to stay a little longer."

"No, I prefer that you are gone when my death comes. I've instructed Conrad to burn my remains and throw my ashes into the river."

"Are you afraid of dying, again?"

"Yes, a little."

"Do you believe in heaven?"

"I believe in you."

"When I die, will I drift in darkness?"

"You'll return to where you were before you were born."

"Do you think I might go to hell?"

"Hell? Ha! You shouldn't worry about going to hell. You grew up in Estill County, didn't you?"

Both gazed into each other's eyes wondering if the other was not a dream.

"Without you, I'll be all alone."

"Everyone is alone, Ed. The difference in life is how well we handle that loneliness."

Chapter Seventy Three

Pickled Beet Dawn

All week long a scorcher, the hottest weather Kentucky had ever known; way too hot to stay inside the walls of prison feeling yourself cook and lay around gawking at nothing but each other; the sun had drained the color out of everything it touched leaving its fry footprint of faded gold behind.

Duke had been allowing some guards and prisoners alike to spend much of their days on the river. They would shuck their shoes when they hit the sand along the beach on the river; ah-h, toes in the shady sand was everything, escape--forget it. Back up the hill on the road to the prison the dirt had baked into a powder.

Nobody had seen the warden or Ed all night. But word was not to worry; them two had disappeared to drown their sorrows; some rotten soul had stolen the warden's counterfeit along with the plates. You couldn't trust nobody, not even an inmate; worst still, Ed was leaving; he had managed stay a little longer, promising Duke that he'd leave on his eighteenth birthday.

And now that day was here, July 11, 1854.

Ed stood watching the drawbridge be lowered. Across the penitentiary's moat, a blackbird with red shoulders was messing in the cattails, fussing at a snake eyeing one of his mates' nests which owned four partially-speckled, blue eggs. In the middle of the prison yard atop the flagpole, a solid red rooster greeted the dawn; many eyes had studied that bird for a meal but he was always spared as he was the warden's pet.

Ed raised his arms all but spellbound as he gazed up into a deep red almost purple sky.

All week he and Duke had been throwinback, drowning that eventual forever goodbye. They'd defeated the summer heat by finding solitude in a secret room located under the prison's dungeon; down a winding staircase to what some claimed was originally an old torture chamber. After Duke became the warden the only torture ever occurring in that room was when some poor person had to leave; the chamber was stacked in red painted crates marked "FRANCE." Every crate was packed with red labeled brandy, contraband from the French Revolution captured off Napoleon at Waterloo; at least, that was the story; How the stuff ever got to Kentucky, nobody know-d; Duke's only comments was, it proved there was a God, even if happened to be French.

Sometime before dawn, Ed and Duke had opted to emerge from the torture chamber finding a drinking roost aloft in the watchtower; a tender breeze, fat moon and stars greeted them; the prison yard was sound asleep.

When dawn broke the sky was the same color as a pickled beet.

Off in the distance Duke and Ed could see the dust of a carriage rising along a ridge at an uncommon pace.

Ed soon walked down the steps going out of the prison.

Duke looked on from the tower, flipping ashes.

Ed throwdback. Standing on one leg, he rubbed his foot up and down against the back of his leg, polishing his boot, anticipating the possibility of hitching a ride.

Conrad woke up and rubbed his red eyes and then snuck in a quick throwdback; he was leaning on the front wall near the ramp close to where the big cogged wheels that controlled the drawbridge; he had been made a head guard because he stood a head taller than anybody; the only thing he ever really guarded was the torture chamber, making sure nobody broke in, except himself; the gate had been down all night.

Chapter Seventy Four

Good Morning Heartache

Fast horses were approaching.

The whole prison could hear the hard "thlot-thlots."

Then, the sound stopped.

As the dust settled, there before Ed was a red carriage and four red thoroughbreds.

Silence momentarily reigned and then, the only breeze having stirred in two weeks began to stir.

The door of the carriage opened. "Boy, come hyur!" ordered a red face.

Ed walked past a butterfly still resting from the night; its lower brown wings exposed a pattern remindful of two red eyes. There, sitting in the back of the carriage was Judge Quinn. Ed turned and looked back at the front wall; Conrad's curly head was looking straight at him.

"You look good," spoke the Judge. "Taller than you were two years ago."

"You're out a far piece from Irvine, ain't-cha," searched Ed, turning his head back around.

"Not so far when it's something important. I lost my deputy to a Pea Ridge back-shooter. I didn't know how to replace him and then I remembered you. Found out today was your last. Remember giving me your word two years ago about being my deputy?"

"Not to change the subject, but what's that you're drinkin'?"

"I call it, 'Ravenna Rainwater,' a blend of t'maters and moon. Reverend Redworm from Red River concocted this red delight. He claims it will put you in heaven."

"I ain't had a single drink in over two years."

Judge Quinn reached under his seat and gave Ed a quart. "A man's word is his worth, I always say, you agree?"

"What about what a man owns, like himself, ain't that got nothin' to do with his worth?"

The Judge reached over into a leather bag and withdrew a jar, knifing out a pickled beet dripping with its sweet juices. "You know what peacemakers do, don't-cha?"

"Inherit the earth?"

The Judge swallowed his beet. "That's correct. And the better a man is at peacemakin' the better he'll inherit. Play your cards right, wear my deputy's star, and you'll inherit this."

Chapter Seventy Five

Such a Weight

Ed watched as Judge Quinn unfolded his hand, revealing a red agate. "This came to me a few months ago," informed the Judge. "It was found on Catfish Creek. Ever see anything any prettier?"

The agate owned a powerful spell.

In its center was a chevron pattern made up of swirls of red, black and yellow that oddly outlined a buzzard's head.

"It's sure a sweetheart," remarked Ed. "But it's way too heavy for me. I could never pack such a weight."

The Judge swallowed another beet, throwdback and smiled. "I've got two sugar-cured hams hanging back home, forty pounders; been soaking sorghum since last November, just coming outta the June sweat, yours under the right conditions."

Ed smacked his lips. "The past two years has reformed me," he confessed. "All I want in the way of peacemakin' is to find peace within myself."

Quinn began moving his right hand carefully along his chest.

"If I was you," advised Ed, "I wouldn't be reaching for something stupid like a hidden pistol. If you'll look along the wall you'll see a brass framed, fifty-four caliber, Eli Whitney Mississippi rifle trained on you. That's my good friend, Conrad, looking over the sights; he can hit a sparrow at one hundred yards, he can't miss at this range."

Quinn peered along the wall and saw something shiny reflecting in his direction. He eased his hand back down, watching, as Duke walked across the bridge, then stopped; he was wearing a pair of dark blue sunglasses that he'd gotten from the doctor.

"Howdy," spoke the Judge.

"Any trouble, here?" asked Duke holding a sawed-off, eight gauge shotgun, his flock decimator, the gun normally used to supply the prison with ducks and geese.

"No trouble," smiled Ed. "This man made a trip all the way from Estill County to tell me that the Judge over there has granted me full amnesty, forever. That is what you were saying, isn't it?"

Judge Quinn stared over at the shotgun. "That's right," he responded, moving his head in agreement. "He also asked me to tell you something else. It's Canepole. Two weeks ago, he was found face down, floating in the river."

Chapter Seventy Six

Pain of Reality

Ed was bluer than a burnt beet.

Now with Moses and Canepole gone he sought refuge along the river.

The river had always been his other mother; he admired how she came out of the mountains to go to an ocean he had never seen. Canepole always said of her, "She wants to go home and there's nothing that can stop her. The things that she can give you weigh more than what she takes."

He has always been such a great waterdog, how could he have drowned?

Ed didn't want to think about anything bad about Canepole but he couldn't help it.

There had been times when Canepole would get drunk and hurt whoever was near, especially the family, even Molly, saying horrible things as the whiskey found that empty hole in his heart; the mountains would lean the wrong way and he would bust up anything to straighten them back out. When he was perfectly drunk he would always tell you that nobody was poorer than him. Nobody had ever had a tougher life. And at some point he would beat on his chest and say that he was the smartest man in the world. When you die the worms eat you, he'd rant, certain his pain of reality was shared.

Despite everything, Canepole and summers on the river had been paradise.

Ed loved him.

Chapter Seventy Seven

Through The Dirt

Ed stood there looking down at the fresh hump of dirt and pieces of grey shale on a knoll not far from home; on top of the grave stood a large cane pole, his favorite.

Ed remembered the last time that he and Canepole had been together; it had been cold that day, sometime in November and they were on the river. They had cut across a bend and found themselves at the base of a cliff that was thick with perched buzzards; the lowest-n's no higher than arm's reach; bunches of them had their wings poke-spread, stretching nearly five feet, hoping to catch the sun's first bits of warmth and drying-out; Some were already sunned-up and out patrolling for death. Up close at the water's edge the fog kept breaking up as it swirled and waltzed on the river; sometimes it came toward them, passing through them and then disappearing.

Had it been a sign?

It was hard to talk to your father through the dirt; nothing so proved that life was an illusion as a grave.

The thought consumed Ed.

Bending over, he placed a Jew's harp at the base of the cane. Then he stood and moved his hand through the warm air.

Nothing was there.

For the longest spell he lay on the grave, weeping as the Whippoorwills dissolved into Hoot Owls

Chapter Seventy Eight

Rub My Back

Ed walked home.

For the first time since birth all of his brothers and sisters and mother were under the same roof.

That late evening Ed found himself stretched on a cattail mattress close to his mother. The glow of the coals from the chimney induced a reflective mood; most everyone was trained on that fireplace; cherry logs still a little green glowed orange against each other as they sizzled and popped in the stillness.

After a spell, some talkin' come.

"I watched dad put away three jugs in three days once; One minute singin' sad, the next, a-wantin' to fight."

"Last summer he took him a big run and went head first off Buzzard Point. After he hit, I didn't see nothin' fer five minutes. When he come up, he had a mussel in one hand and a bottle in the other."

"Me and Birdlegs see-d him shoot the narrows and go straight out over the falls. Birdlegs allowed he'd hate to be in that canoe with Canepole. And I told him, I'd sure hate to be in there without him."

"I was bad a-feared somethin' like this was gonna happen. People have never believed in that catfish but I knew he was there."

"Tomorrow, I say we all go to Irvine, buy up all the gun powder and blast that catfish to hell."

"Doc Ginny allowed, what she warn't positive the body were dad's. Nobody could swear on nothin' the way it looked. She allowed, she were givin' up on Bible stories. Said, no Jonah could-a lived in no whale after she see-d what she see-d."

"I can never forget all the times he used to rub my back."

"Me too."

Molly attempted to get up out of her bed, raising upright as she wiped away the dried mucous having formed at the corner of her mouth; she tried in vain to talk as she'd been drunk all week and was drunker still; a slight smile, a grimace, appeared over her face when she realized Ed was close.

Ed felt remorse while rubbing her back. "Mom, I love you," he whispered. "I'm sorry I haven't been a better son. I should have stayed on the farm instead of venturing off. Maybe things would have been different."

"You don't owe no apology," answered Molly. "You were never cut out to be no farmer."

Chapter Seventy Nine

Brothers in a Tree

An hour before daylight, Ed stood dressed and ready to leave.

The Hawkins' black cats had followed him out to an old pine whose top half had snapped in an ice storm; they ran frizzed up the tree, going out onto limbs to be near where Ed had climbed.

Ed bent low, trying to light the last half of his kif cigar; he needed the hemp much more than the tobacco.

Soon, his soul became adrift.

Beside him, the smoke relaxed his feline friends.

Then, here come William climbing up the tree. "What-cha doin'?" he asked.

"Wonderin'."

"On what?"

"Why there's ever a dawn. Why dark is ever divided. Why we ever breathe in this dream."

"You fixin' to leave?"

"I'd like to stay and be near mom, but can't, Judge Quinn."

"Where you headin'?"

"Don't know. Wherever. Where would you go?"

"West, out in Kansas Territory, to a place called, Hall's Hole. There's gold there. Before our government took over, the miners were getting rich. I hear they're paying big money for mules and donkeys; you can get rich even selling whiskey. The Fort Leavenworth guards are now watching over on everything. If you could get on as one of them you might do yourself some smart money."

Ed released a smoke ring; it expanded toward a mired dawn breaking pink over the mountains. "Reckon they'd have me if I could out-shoot their best guard in a contest?"

"Who knows?"

"I probably should work on what is right, on getting into heaven. But don't-cha reckon, what if-n me or you, or anybody outta Estill County, ever really got to heaven, we'd just wind up getting ourselves kicked out;

If not for pocketin' on them streets of gold, then surely for something else."

Chapter Eighty

The Chinese Junk

Ed won the shooting contest, alright.

The guard that he beat was sergeant Pappy Gould. While Pappy was a hundred yards distance and standing up two beer bottles as targets, Ed managed to re-arrange Pappy's rifle sights without anyone noticing.

And after Ed hit his target and Pappy missed his, Ed was soon made one of the guards that protected what little gold there actually was.

But he never got any opportunity to put his hands on it.

He eventually grew tired of acting like he was some kind of dutiful soldier and deserted to distant Missouri towns under the guise of being a Carlisle Barracks, Pennsylvania recruiting officer; his ploy and explanation to potential recruits being that marauders were attacking Kansas and that the army bad needed help; these recruits he signed always had to give him money.

And that money, as he would so marvelously explain, had to go in on all kinds of good military stuff, including an excellent horse that would be permanently theirs, even after they left the service.

But still, this artful game was not satisfaction enough.

And then came that one melancholy afternoon while he was wandering along the wide Mississippi River; he looked up to see something that he'd never seen before; a Chinese junk sailing in his direction; It had two fully battened sails and when it drew close they lowered and an anchor dropped; there was some figure aboard wearing one of those Chinaman's pointy straw hats.

Chapter Eighty One

Ruth Jean McDougal

The junk was just at that distance where you could watch someone but not speak to them short of hollering.

Ed decided to make camp on the bank and bed down there for the night.

Over on the junk there were some half dozen lanterns; round and giving off a glow of red light.

Ed sometimes looked at them as he was having trouble falling asleep.

Several times through the night he woke up.

And on one occasion, close by in the river, he thought he saw a mermaid; she had stared right at him and then ducked under; never showed again.

Moses had told Ed that he had once been out on the ocean at night and saw a flying fish that was four foot long.

Maybe what I saw was its grandmammy, wondered Ed. I saw her, she saw me, and then she disappeared. It wasn't a dream.

Or was it?

Ed went back to sleep some time before dawn. A few hours later, there was an awful splash waking him.

A figure broke the surface making a hell-of-a leap above the water and then disappeared.

Ed continued looking, seeing nothing.

After a few minutes, he smacked his face and then throwdback.

Again, an awful splash.

The sun's rays now clearly cast its spell upon the river.

There, holding dead still was a stunning image.

Raising an arm, she waved.

The girl ducked under and then surfaced near a large flat rock positioned half way between Ed and the junk; she climbed out rather quickly forming a remarkable nude silhouette; tall, long-waisted and long legged; her frame was lean and her hair fell straight down to her hips. "DO YOU LIKE FISH!" she yelled to Ed.

Do I like fish! "WHO ARE YOU?"

She dove back into the water and swam to the junk. "I AM RUTH JEAN MCDOUGAL FROM BEN NEVIS, THE HIGHEST MOUNTAIN IN SCOTLAND, I AM," she proudly announced in a foreign tongue once on deck. "COME NOW, YOU'VE BONNY WELL STARED ENOUGH! FISH IS BEST WHEN IT'S FRESH!"

Chapter Eighty Two

How America Was Discovered

Ed smiled, took off shoes and shirt then jumped into the river.

When he climbed up on the junk Ruth was dressed in some sort of fancy black and gold plaid that she had brooched to her shoulder and belted around her waist; she was leaned over forward as she ran a comb through her long, dark-red hair; an immense sword was standing near the boom behind her; close by on the deck was a string of blue-gills. "Are you figurin' on cleanin' fish with that?" he joked, nodding towards the sword.

"It's all King Arthur left me."

"King Arthur, huh?"

"You don't believe me, do you? Say, what's your name?"

"Ed."

The two looked hard at each other and laughed; if Miss Chesteen had five thousand freckles Ruth had twice more; each a magnet and Ed made of poor iron.

"Do you have anything like grease, flour, pepper, and a skillet?"

Ruth held tight on Ed's eyes. "Heavens m-n, I wouldn't be much of a cook if I didn't, now would I? I have some green tomatoes in a basket near the sunflowers. You wouldn't care frying them as well, would you?"

"Tell me something, is Scotland heaven?"

"Heaven? You might say that, but real heaven, no, as there be no such place; religion rests with fear and fraud. We McDougals are Highlanders. This time of the year, our world is covered in heather, every glen, a royal purple. I-kun only be there now in my wee mind. We McDougals kun no longer stand the sight of the McClary's. Rather than have their blood on our hands, we left our homeland. Perhaps it's good. Who knows in a world such as ours?"

"How come the McDougals hate the McClarys?"

"Me grandfather, R-R-Russell McClary, died before me grandmother. When that happened, there went all me poor mother's inheritance, considerable, it were. Me mother's two older brothers, both shamefully lazy and spoiled cowards, surrounded me grandmother, Queen Mac, eventually capturing her ninety-year-old soul into their avarice pockets. Family is everything: Blood. It's a pity me uncles were unable to see that. Me mother got nothing when Queen Mac died. Me father, whom was born in a cave along the top of the highest mountain in all Scotland, said we must leave: That to live in hate was no good. Still, I own a certain sense of suffering of which escape be hopeless. Me father had heard about the mountains and fishing in America in a place like Scotland called Kentucky. I hope to go there in wee time. It is what he would have wanted."

"Where is he?"

"Gone."

"Where?"

"He took his own life. All I have now is this wee boat. Don't ever inquire about it as I will never tell."

"How old are you?"

"Twenty-five I am, September twenty-seventh born, in a place overlooking the Steall Falls in Glen Nevis; Me father 'n brothers were fishing on River Nevis at the time, not to be blamed, the salmon were running."

"I was born when my brothers were fishing, too."

"Me father told me, 'when you are born in the last week of September you become that person that owns the heart of summer and knows that winter is near.'"

"I was born on July eleventh. Mom claimed, 'being born in the middle of summer spoils a child.' Those salmon, are they any good to eat?"

"A marvelous fish, they are; Great fighters; Delicious pink meat. It's best to catch them just as they come from the sea, especially in icy water.

Plenty of fat, they have then. When you catch one, your day is complete."

"Did you know that if it weren't for fishing, the United States would have never been discovered?"

"And how is that?"

"If Christopher Columbus hadn't-a gotten lost while fishin' him and his bunch would never have discovered America."

"It was a good mistake, was it not?"

"Maybe, but the Indians sure didn't think so."

271

"What were you doing along the river, yesterday? I watched you from my scope and you seemed content on going nowhere."

"Nowhere, I'll have you know, I am a bona fide panther hunter, the very best. I've been hired direct by Mr. P. T. Barnum and Seth Howes to rid black panthers off the earth. P.T. figures a hundred or more got loose and now is scourin' the Mississippi. The biggess-n I've killed so far was over six foot long, not counting its tail."

"Oh, that's a tale alright."

"When they're all gone, I'm to get ten thousand dollars," allowed Ed, holding lovefied. He had never seen any girl with such smart green eyes, as though those eyes could see right through him and beyond; and her voice was raspy-feminine and intriguing; green and yellow were those eyes, mountain gold, a blend of Junebug dazzle.

"Ten thousand, oh, that would be something, for sure. But who needs money when you've got the river? We need the water to free us from having been born."

"Barnum is counting big on my cleaning up his mistake. He's left it up to me to stop the devouring of young gals; P.T.'s Caravan busted loose upstream in a place called, Estill County; Plum-awful, it were; animals was scattered everywhere. The big apes, baboons and such, all busted loose in Irvine; I caught a bunch of them, but not all, there's still a few running loose in their courthouse. These panthers, well, ain't no ordinary black panthers. They have enormous fangs and feed exclusively on Christians. We'd be further upstream, only there is no need, if there are any Christian eating panthers up that way, they're surely gone, died-off from starvation. Next to giant catfish, black panthers are the worstess thang there are."

"Oh-h, I doubt that. The most horrible matter one can face is rough seas in the middle of the night. I'll take your panthers any time verses that. The voices I hear inside me head say there are no shores, that we are destined to drift among the eternities, unknown and of no consequence."

How did she ever learn to sail a boat like this, wondered Ed; everything in his past fell flat by the wayside. She went into her cabin for a few minutes and when she came back out she had that sword and smelled just like honeysuckle. When she got close, Ed leaned forward a notch and gave her a quick kiss on her lips.

Ruth didn't know what to think, but she didn't object; she was just as impulsive as him.

Chapter Eighty Three

And Forever Would Be

It was cold that October morning, the first frost of the year and a hard one.

Ed and Ruth hadn't left each other's sides since they'd met; sailing up the Mississippi River to the Ohio River and then stopping near Louisville to lock through onto the Kentucky River while waving at steamers and catching so many fish was an incredible experience.

But now Ed's toes were cold; he was sleeping on his stomach in the junk's cabin where he and Ruth always slept.

Something got a hold of his eye and made them slightly open.

And then he shut them again.

He rolled over and began to feel that Ruth wasn't there.

Slowly, he rose up.

And then his heart completely stopped.

What is a nightmare when no nightmare?

There, through the open door, nude with her feet just barely off the ground, her head oddly cocked, hanging ghastly dead, was all of Ed's dreams in one; Ruth's eyes were open, glazed, staring straight at him.

276

Ed had her tender down in a second; trembling, he kissed, breathed and hugged on her until he collapsed, wailing, crying aloud as never before in his life. "PLEASE DON'T BE DEAD! PLEASE DON'T BE DEAD--Oh God, why me!"

It was too late.

All that was real was gone.

Ed continued to bawl, his body beside hers.

He raised and looked down at her; his heart was pounding. "WHY! WHY ME!" he shouted up to the sky, uncontrollably crying.

Then he bent over, shut her eyes and lifted her body. As he began to carry her he tripped over a bucket, falling, hitting his head and losing consciousness.

When he came to, the sun was cresting the mountain on the other side; a jagged shadow covered two thirds of the water's surface; he touched the knot having swollen on his head.

For a moment Ed wanted to leave the world; he stepped off the junk and walked over to the river's edge; there, in the still water just below the surface were rows of tiny ridges in the sand.; a red leaf came by; it changed course and ever so slow came by again.

In and out, breathed Ed, full of wonder, fear, doubt and dream.

He hated existence.

The horror of Ruth's death returned.

Who said, God is merciful?

Ed felt infinitely hollow, something other than alive; he did not know if he was strong enough to go on.

He went back onto the junk and carried her body back into their cabin. Then he laid her on the bed and gently kissed her before covering her in her family's plaid. He stepped back and after a spell finally sat down beside her; from his dark corner he felt her death was somehow his fault. "Why God, why?" he cried.

The dead hear nothing.

Life is hideous.

Outside, the colorful fall woods were being shadowed by the most graceful bird in the world, the eater of dreams.

Ed rose, set the cabin on fire and left.

When at last he topped a ridge, he looked back; smoke was rising from the river valley.

As evening fell, geese were calling in the black sky.

Winter was coming.

For Ed, winter was here, and forever would be.

Chapter Eight Four

Chigger

About the only good thing that happened for Ed throughout that following bad winter was that most of the chiggers had died.

--But not all of them.

Once spring snuck back around and Kentucky started eating sunshine those irritating creatures took to stirrin' once more.

Bad they were, almost as bad as rats.

The river attracted rats and those rats were always stirring, especially in Irvine, Kentucky. One of the two-legged rats was a scrawny, bow-legged figure called, "Chigger." Chigger Chainy to be correct.

Chigger operated the ferry on the river that led back and over to Irvine.

Chigger didn't make much money.

But it kept him in whiskey.

"I'm rich!" he caterwauled, rushing pell-mell into The Wigwam; in his hands was Estill County's newspaper, THE GOLDEN EAGLE; its masthead depicted an eagle soaring over the river; beneath the depiction in bold print was the motto: WHERE THE BLUEGRASS KISSES THE MOUNTAINS AND THE TRUTH STAYS AT HOME.

Jim Land, Judge Quinn's scurrilous sheriff of Estill County, and his weasel deputy, Jessie Arvin, were having a drink and playing poker when Chigger dropped the newspaper on their table; neither of the officials appreciated Chigger interrupting their game, particularly sheriff Land as he was holding four aces. "Rich," he mocked Chigger. "That'll be the day."

"Look at it," insisted Chigger. "I ain't-a lyin' none!"

Sheriff Land folded his hand, taking the paper. "BEWARE" he read aloud. "By The Colonel. Tomorrow is March 15, 1857. Back in them old Roman days, March 15 was something bad. And as I see it, every day is March 15—"

"No, no!" interrupted Chigger. "Fergit that stuff," he ranted. "It's the back page! Read that big ree-ward notice: The one advertisin' fifty dollars!"

Sheriff Land turned the paper around; down near the bottom was a squared-off sketch of a horse. "Fifty dollars reward," he announced.

"That's it, go on, read the rest!"

"I, Owen Kerr, president of The Richmond People's Bank, will pay fifty dollars to anyone bringing me my black mare or the thief that stole her. She disappeared from my stables on March 12, sometime late Saturday night. She is 15 hands tall, sleek, calm, and has my brand 'OK.' Of note, she is afraid of water."

"I saw that mare yesterday," informed Chigger. "I know who had her and where he was goin'. They was on my ferry."

"Are you sure?"

"Ed Hawkins was his name, black hair; about six foot, blue-eyed. He said he was headed to Proctor. I made mention on the horse and he told me he won her playin' poker. It'll be an easy fifty dollars."

"Got 'er all figured out, don't-cha?"

"Sixteen dollars and sixty-six cents fer each of us."

"Jesse, what's your say on this?"

"Let's go get him. We ain't doing nothing here."

"Chigger, do you swear to uphold my laws and do exactly what I tell you?"

"I do."

"Then I deputize you as our third man out in charge of this expedition. Jesse, get Chigger a gun. And throw a saddle on Sweet Tater."

"Who's going to work the ferry for Chigger?"

"It'll have to run itself. Last time I was gone I left a bucket for donations. When I come back, there warn't even no bucket!"

Chapter Eighty Five

Three Sixes

The next morning Ed was on the river bank pulling in a fish when the three lawdogs from Estill County appeared, introducing themselves, later mentioning the stolen horse; beside Ed was a book with a poem in it called, The Raven, and a few feet on over was Jenny, his mare.

"I won her off Owen Kerr's son, Owen Jr.," explained Ed. "He's ashamed to tell his dad what happened; Him bettin' her on three sixes and me a-holdin' three aces. I'll tell Owen, senior what happened. I just hope Owen Jr. owns up to the fact."

"Just come back to Irvine. If we bring you in, we get fifty dollars, that's all we care. You and Mr. Kerr and his son can work it all out. In a couple of days, you can be right back fishing. The way they've been biting, I might come with you."

Chapter Eighty Six

Hollow Bones

Thirty days inside an egg.

Seven weeks in the nest.

Then flight.

A lifespan of over 100 years.

A six feet wingspan.

A broad "V" silhouette,

Floating on updrafts of air.

Air being heated at ground level.

Floating in those pockets of air.

Rising on the currents.

Floating in a circle.

Staying within the pocket of air.

Smelling.

Searching.

Floating from one pocket to another.

Observing.

Circling.

Hollow boned.

A life of feast and famine.

A life of quiet.

A life much alone.

Below, the eater of dreams watched the lawdogs and Ed sail empty whiskey bottles off a cliff; it was the second time they'd done so.

The sun was straight up and all of them were drunk.

Or so it seemed as the huckleberry Ed had been putting on a quite good act; one in which he hadn't touched a drop...

Chapter Eighty Seven

The Winding Staircase

Came noon, way high were an ol' buzzard; so very high, sometimes disappearing behind the clouds; a winged snake that thang were, descended from his great, great granddaddy what had feasted on ol' Ceaser hisself, Brutus too. Down below, finished empties was again bein' throw-d off a cliff; the lawdogs shot at them bottles but nobody could hit nothin', they all was too drunk, 'cept Ed; drunk, too, he acted; drunk and havin' hisself a good ol' time with his new buddies. But one thing was secret-certain, he warn't about to go back and face no Judge Quinn.

"Pass that last pint over here, Jesse, and I'll tell you about an old buzzard. How if it weren't for him, we wouldn't have any mountains or anything. Gentlemen, back when the world was a ball of mud, God sent a giant buzzard to swoop low. The ridges and things are where the mud squashed up through that buzzard's wings. God cried after He saw how sweet things turned out; his tears became the Kentucky River; she's the only thing that runs true through Estill County, and even she is pretty crooked."

Riding on to the top of a steep mountain trail called, The Winding Staircase, Jim's and Ed's horses stopped dead even; Jesse's and Chigger's mounts were right behind.

Ed had been waiting all day for such a moment.

He knew he'd have one chance and one chance only to save his life.

All in one motion, he grabbed Jim's right hand with his left. As he did, he reached across with his right arm and withdrew Jim's pistol that was exposed under his coat in his shoulder holster.

It happened so fast.

A shot went to Jim's head.

Then, two more shots echoed from the mountain.

Chapter Eighty Eight

Oblique Dimensions

Ed was hearing the strange sounds of a cicada symphony in the woods; a constant buzzing that seemed to increase and abrade his thoughts.

I wish they would stop.

A pink sunset stained with blood captured the sky, forest and Ed's soul; he crouched low, horseless, balancing on a moss covered stump, afraid; all around him were crow scouts calling to their flock; the black spirits were dropping from the pink sky, roosting oddly close in a silent council; among the laurel and rhododendron, the queer twilight arrested the woods in a transcendent realm where all remained somber in a pink theatre of oblique dimensions. As the pink began to fade, Ed held his hands in front of his face. Did I murder three men?

He could not control the tremble in his heart as tears streamed down his face. He could still see Chigger begging him for his life before he had shot him through his left eye. As darkness fell so did so many stars.

For a moment he thought he heard something, he wasn't sure.

Then he heard it again; the cry of a hounds; one was closer than the others.

They're dead on my trail, he noted, maybe ten or twelve minutes off, running hard. He looked off into the darkness trying to grab his bearings; the river was out there somewhere. If he could get to it, it would run back to Irvine. He turned and looked at the shadowy mountain ridges between him and his home; somewhere past those ridges below the North Star was Molly.

He began running and then slowed down, smart-pacing himself as his eyes adjusted to the blackness; coming to a cliff he paused; the dogs were closing ground; he stepped back and leap-jumped into the top of a tree, hitting hard, then climbed down making it to a creek; it was wide and swollen; really more of a small river than a creek. There was no way to know how deep it was and to cross it was impossible; straight up above on the cliff's edge a hound arched its neck and howled.

Ed looked toward his pursuer and then searched for the North Star; the moon's light throw-d some help as he stayed his course side-stepping from rock to rock. A ways further, he began to hear the dogs again; flesh concentrating on flesh, holding keen onto his smell, five, maybe six minutes back.

Chapter Eighty Nine

Slippery Gamble

Ed kept running until he hit a place where he had to either climb up a steep mountain or go across the creek; he only had seconds to make the decision as the hounds had steadily been closing ground. If I try to go up that mountain they'll get me, he guessed.

As soon as he stepped into the water he knew there was no turning back; the numbing cold sent a shock to his feet. Please don't be over my head, he prayed, wading out deeper.

The water began taking Ed's breath and the under current was powerful, all you could do to move one leg at a time through it without being swept away; and each step a slippery gamble of life or death.

At mid-way in the stream Ed all but went under as he fought to gain balance. After he did he continued taking one crucial step after another until making it over. Once there on the rocky other side, he found himself frozen with leg cramps, straining to take more steps before collapsing and then crawling to hide behind a boulder; just as he did a dog on the other side began to cry. A few minutes later, the other dogs were barking; their tails were pointing up and out and in every direction as their angled bodies sniffed the ground; two of them were black and tan, the leader was solid red; soon followed the men with their lanterns, stopping to study the dogs and the area, shooting wildly throughout the woods with one bullet ricocheting close to Ed's position.

"Do you think he crossed the creek?

"He might've tried but that was as far as he could have got."

"Come on, he has to be on down. If we can get up that mountain fast enough we'll catch him on the other side."

"You sure?"

"Look at the dogs; he hit the water, alright."

"If he's downstream, he won't be alive, a man wouldn't last a minute in that water."

"You're probably right, but you never know. We need his body. We can't collect on the reward without it."

Chapter Ninety

North Star

Ed watched as the lanterns went back up the mountain. There was a chance they might double back. But the longer he held still the stiffer he was becoming. He raised and began to climb the steep mountain behind him as he needed to gain distance from his hunters and locate his position.

When he reached the top of the mountain he came out into a large clearing. His body heat from the constant movement had considerably dried him out. He looked up into a brilliant sky filled with stars. And there, at the end of the constellation he knew as the Great Bear, at the end of its tail, was the North Star; it was not the brightest star but it was by far the most important. Home by daybreak, maybe, he thought, got to keep moving.

Ed angled off the mountain and was soon sitting and sliding on his rear to keep from falling. At one point he stopped as he had slid upon a small tree that came in between his legs. It was black dark and at the moment he stopped and he sensed the air was different, lighter and icy. And then his eyes adjusted to the night. Oh God, he trembled. I've slid out on to the edge of a cliff, a hundred foot straight drop.

He began inching back up the mountain, leaning backwards while digging in his heels and holding on to roots until he could go back down another route. When he made it back down into the hollow he walked to the creek.

What? He wondered, perplexed.

It took him a minute to figure out what had happened; He was now downstream from where he had first crossed, at a place where the creek forked. This realization all but consumed his spirit as he now knew that he would have to cross the creek twice more if he wanted to make it home.

Don't think on it, just do it.

It took all of his willpower but he crossed both creeks. Again, he was soaked wet, numb and exhausted.

If I stop, I'm dead.

As he began his struggle up the next mountain he unluckily proceeded into a monstrous briar thicket. The merciless thorns punctured his face, hands, legs and ears until he had no choice but to turn around, folding his self in a protective way, and then fighting one backward step at a time until he reached the top, came to a rock fence and collapsed; the frosted weeds crunched and stuck to him.

And sooner did he curl onto the ground, unable to move, than he felt something breathing on his neck.

Chapter Ninety One

Blood to Be With Blood

In the cloak of darkness a yet darker spirit appeared.

"Jenny, is that you?"

Jenny had scattered with the other horses when Ed fell backwards during the shooting. It took every ounce of strength he owned to get up and ease onto her back; her body warmed him; a hoot owl hollered; the North Star was still there.

An hour later, he rode up to a cabin. "HELLO," he shouted, "IS ANYBODY IN THERE!"

"I AIN'T A-LETTIN' YOU IN, NED HAWKINS! I DONE HYEER-D ON YOU! YOU IS A MURDERIN' HORSE THIEF! EVEN IF YOU PAWNED YOR HONOR, YOU AIN'T WEL-COME, I'VE GOT A GUN!"

Ed left.

The worser the news the worser it traveled in Estill County.

Ed rode near the Fitchburg Furnace; the sixty feet high massive stone-block structure was being built to smelt raw iron into pig iron; soon the workers living near it would be awake. If I go that one way, remembered Ed. It's a short cut.

Blood to be with blood.

Home.

At just before daylight, Ed sat on the floor, his hands in Molly's lap. "Tell me it's a bad dream, mom."

Molly drew Ed in close, slipping her fingers though his hair, remembering the day he was born.

"Those three bringing me in left me no choice. The horse that I got caught with is the same mare I traded to get dad out of jail. After I did that, I stole her back. Judge Quinn would've hung me if they had brought me in. Owen Kerr and his son -- that ain't their real names-- those two are some of the bunch that knocked me in the head and left me for dead when I was robbing Quinn's store for wages he owed me and wouldn't pay. That's what wound me up in the pen. Mom, I wish I were dead. Tell me, what do you want me to do?"

Tears were coming down Molly's cheeks. "Nancy," she ordered. "Go fetch him a ham and fill a sack with cornbread and onions. Put your daddy's old hat in there, too, the one he never wore."

Ed watched as Molly took off the coat that was once Canepole's and laid it over his shoulders. "Mom, you need the coat more than me, please keep it."

"Nonsense. I have your love to keep me warm. Put it on. If you get to safety don't look back. I love you. You are my blood. Son, this isn't a dream. If they catch you, they'll hang you. If worse comes to worse, shoot it out. Don't let them take you alive. Swear you will do this and give me one last kiss. I love you. No matter what happens, we'll always be together."

Ed's weary eyes were streaming tears. "I swear," he pledged, and then he gave her a kiss on her forehead and both cheeks. He pulled out Sheriff Land's 1855 Colt Root revolver and then took the sack from Nancy. "I love you, too," he said, pulling back the spur trigger, checking the cylinder; there were two rounds left but the powder had gotten wet.

Nancy began to sob while hugging Ed. "If you let them sons-o-bitches catch you, I'll never forgive you."

Ed held Nancy for a long time and then broke off and walked out to Jenny to see that the sun was up.

Molly stood at the door. "You know that birthmark you've got on your belly?" she asked. "The other person that has it is Moses, you might ponder that. Now listen. If they catch you they'll surely torture you before they hang you. You ride smart."

Ed mounted Jenny and watched as Nancy took Molly's hand. "I'm goin' north, Mom. You tell them that when they come. Tell them the truth because they'll know you're lying."

A minute later Ed was gone.

Chapter Ninety Two

Too Tired To Dream

Evening.

Ed and Jenny were give out.

They'd found a cliff overhang for refuge.

For nearly twenty miles they had artfully dodged one posse after another; twice, Ed had spotted reward posters offering five hundred dollars for his return, dead or alive. At one place he heard a bunch closing in on him and he jumped off Jenny, hid her, and then put on Canepole's coat and hat, acting like he was a feeble, old man repairing a stone fence. When the bunch rode up he told them that he had earlier seen "a young fellar riding wild on a black mare heading straight south."

Ed fed Jenny his cornbread as he took a bite of raw ham. "No fire tonight, darling," he whispered. "We can't attract the wolves," he explained, thankful the cliff was dripping water as they were both bad thirsty. "You got me in this mess," he told her, gently rubbing her face.

"No, you didn't, I did. I can't be mad at-cha. Twice you've saved my life."

He pondered on what Molly had said about his birthmark.
What did she mean about Moses having the same birthmark in the
same place?

As night took over, he curled up, keeping his Colt pistol in his hand
and falling straight on to sleep too tired to dream.

Chapter Ninety Three

Surrounded

When Ed woke up, it was already day.

A man was hollering. "COME OUT ED HAWKINS, WE'VE GOT YOU SURROUNDED!"

There was no cave in the back of this overhang.

"GIVE UP NOW OR I'LL SICK MY DOG! I'M COUNTING TO THREE! ONE! TWO!"

Ed cocked his pistol knowing it wouldn't shoot.

"THREE!"

Ed could hear a growling dog crashing through the woods.

Unexpectedly, at the cliff's drip line, came the mad scream of a black panther; the cat leaped down from the hidden cleft along the ledge, sinking its sharp teeth deep into the dog's neck and skull, killing it dead on the spot; the panther had been above Ed ever since he had entered the overhang, hiding and protecting her newborn cubs; muskets fired from every position dropping the cat beside the dog.

"WE'VE GOT YOUR SISTER, NANCY. IF YOU DON'T WANT NO HARM PUT ON HER, COME OUT WITH YOUR HANDS UP!"

Ed snuck a look.

There, through the hemlocks was Nancy's red hair.

Jenny was hobbled and so was Ed's heart.

"WHAT'S IT GONNA BE!"

"I'M COMIN' OUT!" hollered Ed, hiding his pistol, rising with his hands high as he walked into clear view.

For a spell there was silence.

Twelve gunmen came out of the woods from their spread positions, cautiously stepping up to Ed; Among them were Joe Ohr, the best tracker in the state, the Reverend Redworm, Piano Red, Huby, Owen Kerr, Jupiter and Judge Quinn.

Judge Quinn threw a hangman's noose over Ed's neck and stepped back, holding the rope tight. "Strip and fetter him," he ordered. "Then, brand him. He now belongs to Estill County." Quinn handed Jupiter an iron with a big "E" on its end. "After that's done, chain him to my hack, he needs educating on what a Blue Monday is." The Judge uncoiled his whip. "And after his schooling, we'll take him back and give him a fair trial and then hang him. You boys can have your way with Nancy, just don't kill her."

Chapter Ninety Four

Or So It Seemed

Darkness.

When you see black and there be no black then you see Irvine; that place had not so much kissed the mountains as she had raped them.

Ed's trial had been forty-five days ago.

He was now under guard, shackled to an iron ball inside a six-foot square, windowless log cell in front of the Irvine courthouse. Death no longer owned any scare; it was his one friend.

Today, he awaits hanging, his world has fallen away.

Or so it seemed.

He lay there in his rags, curled on the dirt floor, asleep.

And then he woke up.

His nightmare opened his eyes. In the nightmare, white rattlesnakes were striking at him; he was in his open grave, laying on his back and looking up at his silent friends that were staring emotionless back down at him.

What a dream, he thought, and then smiled.

Why was his heart light?

Chapter Ninety Five

Ed's Trial

Ed moved and sat up against the inner wall of his log cell; outside he could hear the sounds of a large crowd. As his mind began to roam he remembered back to forty-five days ago to that carnival-like ordeal that was called his trial; it seemed as if it had happened only moments ago…Into Irvine had journeyed the whole blessed county, from The Devil's Backbone, Poosey Ridge, Fightin' Branch, Crooked Creek, Crystal, Willow, Beattyville Mountain, Dry Ridge, Wisemantown, Trottin' Ridge, Cedar Grove, Bear Wallow, Possum Run, Pitts, Woolly Ridge, Winston, Turkey Foot, Alexander Hollow, Sand Hill, Drip Rock, Miller's Creek, Knob Lick, Pea Ridge, Rice Station, Old Landing, Middle Fork, Sugar Hollow, Hickory Hills, Fox, Doe Creek, Muddy Creek, Leeco, Red Lick, Sweet Lick, Hargett, Happy Top, Ravenna,

Furnace, Marble Yard, White Oak, Cressy, Pryse, Red River, Old Pike, Cobb Hill, Sally Ann Mountain, Station Camp, Ticky Fork, Dry Branch, Sand Gap, Owl Hollow, Brushy Mountain, The Pinnacle, Cave Hollow, Cow Creek, Rudco Ridge, Drowning Creek, Wagersville, Chestnut Stand, Spout Springs, Dark Hollow and everywheres that was anywheres.

Estill County's inhabitants were packed in tight around Irvine's courthouse; whiskey was flooding the Wigwam as the magnificent Judge Quinn came strutting out and smiling at the sky as he proceeded down Main Street in some kind of Mexican general's black and gold uniform jacket owning a blue and white cloak flowing over his brass epaulets; atop his head he donned a powdered wig; the medal he'd won was shining on his chest; it being second in attention to his knee-high boots with rooster headed spurs; the scabbard of his Ames wristbreaker drug the ground and the belt that he was wearing had a gold-gilded buckle showing Kentucky's state symbol: two men shaking hands; he was carrying a quart of whiskey, a Bible, a law book, a coiled whip and an ox shoe; the one he liked to use for his gavel.

Before the beginning of the event some bald headed, fat man wearing thick glasses, calling himself, Larry Kelly, sat down whatever he was smoking and stood up at the front and hollered: "HERE YE! HERE YE! THE HONORABLE JUDGE ABNER QUINN IS NOW TAKING OVER! HIM AND ME GO BACK TO WHEN THIS PLACE WARN'T

NOTHIN'! HE'S A REAL HOUND DOG, HE IS! A TRUE HERO! LAST ELECTION I VOTED FOR HIM FIVE TIMES! NOW, I WANT EVERBODY TO SHUT UP! THE JUDGE WANTS THIS THING TO BE FAIR AND ALL THAT STUFF!"

One witness, Junebug S. Johnson, staggered to the stand smoking what he always smoked – cannabis stuff he grew on the river at his "Skeeter Ranch" -- swearing that he "was a-diggin' sang when he seed all the terrible killin'." Estill County knew the high probability that

Junebug hadn't see-d nothin' but a bottle in over twenty years.

Another witness, Buster Rawlins, known as "Buck," a pockmarked faced, mammoth of a human, wholly illiterate, born dirt poor and gone downhill from there, came to the stand in new blue clothes much too small for him wearing a pair of blue sunglasses; he stunk up the courtroom as his smell flourished throughout in the search for a chair that would fit him; he sat down his jug and a jar of pickled corn, swearing-in wrong-handed while chewing tobacco; He was challenged to swear to tell the truth, and nothing but the truth, so help him God. Buster listened to all that and then spit. He allowed that he were from Irvine. And that "nobody from Irvine had ever done sech a thang." But that he'd give it a try. Then, he took and swore, he'd "drank more corn, eat more corn and grow-d less corn than any man they'd avur been." That's when everyone bust out laughing and Quinn had to set his bottle down, pounding his bench with that ox shoe, then raising and popping that whip, and next, shooting off the pistol that was being used as the evidential murder weapon in order to promote silence. Buster throwdback. And then, in his squeaky voice, he said that was the "first-n to come on the murderin' place. Awful, it were; Them three had been robbed clean. When I got to Chigger, that scrawny thang uttered it were that Ed Hawkins what done it all."

Quinn smiled and then took a big throwdback. He informed Ed there was a gentleman sitting behind him that was offering to represent him; Do it for free. As far as Quinn cared, it was fine by him. The man was some lawyer half lost, horribly mis-directed and passing through. "Lincoln, is his name. Abraham Lincoln."

Ed remembered turning and looking; straight behind him, a head taller than anyone else, sat the most melancholy figure he'd ever seen; the man glowed in despair. Ed didn't want any part of him, there was no use dragging something like that into this, he thought.

And then Huby came to the stand, drunker than usual; one of his eyes kept going inward looking at his nose. When he was asked to swear to tell the truth he burst out laughing, stood, and then reached over to get a drink from the Judge's bottle. That's when Nancy yelled out in court, "HE AIN'T GOING TO TELL THE TRUTH! THE TRUTH AIN'T IN HIM AND YOU KNOW IT!"

Judge Quinn got the bottle back from Huby and told him to sit back down. After the Judge had a throwback he looked out at the courtroom and then said, "FOR ALL OF YOU THAT THINK THAT HUBY DOESN"T HAVE A DROP OF GOD IN HIM I AM GOING TO HAVE HIM HYPNOTIZED SO THAT WHAT-EVER HE SAYS WILL GO UNTESTED! WE ALL KNOW THAT YOU CAN ONLY TELL THE TRUTH WHEN YOU ARE HYPNOTIZED!"

Huby sat there on the witness stand as Larry Kelly pulled out his gold watch and swung it back and forth in front of his face, telling Hubert that he was "getting sleepy." The courtroom settled down into a perfect silence observing the performance. "You are getting very sleepy," continued Larry Kelly. "You are now asleep."

Hubert's eyes closed. And he sat there asleep for about fifteen seconds before he began to talk in his sleep. "I was huntin' turkey when I saw everything," he slowly announced. "I saw Ed Hawkins tie all three of them to a tree and then laugh as he shot them. He shot at me when I came after him. His horse was too fast and he got away."

Larry Kelly next counted to three, clapped his hands, and said, "Huby, you can now wake up, everything is OK."

Molly then stood up and said, "THIS TRIAL IS NOT FAIR! MY BOY AIN'T GETTING HIS SAY!"

That's when a barefooted, tiny, perfectly muscled, albino black man that was tattooed from head to toe, wearing a beaded and peacock feathered headband, came marching into the courtroom, parting right through the middle of everybody and up to the stand; he had on a grassy skirt thing over some pink silky britches and was smoking a kif cigar; on his shoulder was a big blue and gold parrot and in one hand, a folded, tasseled pink umbrella; Once at the witness stand, he swore himself in, speaking in a delicate and absolute perfect English; the same kind of stuff them English people do. "I am Spartacus," he said, "Chief of all Mbuti Pygmies."

"Where in blazes did you learn to talk," asked the Judge.

Spartacus tilted his umbrella; a stream of light was coming through the window directly at him; as though dipped in several different tones of silver and white, his skin appeared insubstantial, ethereal. "Sir," he informed the courtroom. "I was once married to Miss Elizabeth Hall, an English missionary, having grown lost on an expedition in the Congo. In time, we were soon blessed with the most perfect marriage, sweet beyond all compare, until a day when the slavers came and cap- tured myself and my entire tribe. We endured a boat ride to America, the land of the free; such as I shall never forget...My next matter of consequence was a Mr. John Hunt Morgan selling me to Ben Lark, the Judge of Madison County, Kentucky. Lark later proceeded to take off his wig and attempted to have his way with me. Once he found no co-operation but rather quite the opposite, he then sold me quite cheap to be used as a fox in a rousing foxhunt. For nearly a month before that eventful hunt I was stuffed with cornbread and buttermilk. This measure was performed to assure that my speed upon release would be next to nil. A cage with bells attached to it was eventually chained over my head. When the hunt began, a horn was blown at exactly midnight on July 4th and the shakers and movers of the community allowed me the advance of one hour's head start. One anxious gentleman made a wonderful shot and knocked the bark out from under the limb that I was on and I fell, rolling pell-mell into what I later learned was a groundhog hole. The next morning, quite by accident, I ran up on two gentleman not associated with the hunt that were camped in your Kentucky jungle. These two men managed to remove that ridiculous cage off my head, fed me country ham and eggs, and when my pursu-ers came into their camp, they led them astray with the most delightful story involving their witnessing of my killed-by-a-catfish drowning. God's angels, that's what they were. One of them is the man now on trial, Edward Hawkins." Spartacus pulled out a Bowie. "This is the gift that Ed Hawkins gave me when bidding farewell."

"Are you stating before this court that you are a runaway slave?" questioned the Judge.

"No Sir, not now," answered Spartacus, withdrawing two papers. "The next day after I had been befriended by Ed, as fate would have it, I observed a poor fellow that just happened to be actually drowning. I took the knife given that had been given to me and cut a weeping willow branch that I readily employed in saving the stranger's life. As it so happened, the stranger turned out to be none other than John Hunt Morgan's brother- in- law. Once this life-saving event was well established, Mr. Morgan bought me back only to set me free. These papers I've produced will prove my story."

John Hunt Morgan stood up in the middle of the first row of the balcony and spoke out. "If Ed had not saved Spartacus, my brother-in-law would have drowned--he can't swim a lick. He is the finest person you could ever know, a great father to all his children. This year alone, he has given two thousand dollars to an orphanage in Louisville. I should also inform the court, I took it upon myself to inspect the black mare branded "OK" that is now hitched in front of the Wigwam; the horse that was taken from Ed Hawkins at the time of his capture; She is most definitely the same mare that was stolen from me a few years ago. I would like to know, Mr. Kerr, sir, how did you obtain my horse in the first place?"

Owen Kerr and his son humped up in their seats and lowered their heads without responding.

Then, into the courtroom entered a hog-jawed woman humming "Rock Of Ages;" it was Sister Sally, attempting to act proper; she was clad in calico, wearing a purple bonnet and a dozen strings of different colored Indian beads. When she moved in her prissy manner up to the front where Spartacus was still sitting she said, "Shoo." And she continued to repeat it until she shooed him away from the stand. "My name is Rebecca Bell Hood," she declared. "I'm a good Christian lady that lives up Proctor way. On the night follerin' them murders, I woke up with a knife to my throat. It were none other than Ed Hawkins. He had his way with me; Big bragged on killin' three. Threatened he'd make it four, if I told." She then commenced shaking and bawling.

"Larry, please help that poor lady from my courtroom," ordered Judge Quinn. "Now then, I've got one more witness I've been saving and after he's through, that's it. They ain't gonna be no more arguin', it's time to eat. And after the trial, I'm giving out free whiskey at the Wigwam for as long as it lasts. In the next election I expect all of you to remember where it came from." Quinn pounded his ox shoe. "The court calls Joe Ohr."

Everybody in Estill County knew Joe Ohr as "Hook" because he had a long, hooked nose and was the best of all trackers; once he got on your trail, you were as good as hooked; in appearance he was half weasel and fox mixed together. When he stepped to the stand and had that ragged Bible presented in front of him he attested, "I don't need any book in order to tell the truth, I'm the only honest man in this county and everyone knows it." A hush fell over the courtroom as every bent and buckled bum studied his slant-eyes and hairy ears, straining to hear his low, almost-silent lip-whistling while he tapped his foot and reached inside his brown coat for notes. "The reason I have been called to testify," he asserted, "is to confirm that the trail I followed from the murder scene, led back to Ed. Everyone should know that the Judge instructed me exactly what I was to say and nothing else. I cannot do that. I have always lived by the truth. I have no inten-

312

tions of changing now. When I was first recruited, I was asked to track down a horse thief and murderer. I was told that I would get a share of a $500 reward. I thought that what I was doing was good. Now, after learning what I know, I don't want any share of the reward, not a cent." Hook looked at the envelope he held in his hands and paused--silence owned the courtroom--he read, "ED HAWKINS, ESTILL COUNTY" and then opened the letter inside continuing...

"Dear Ed,

I've been searching for you high and low. You are my angel that God sent to me. Nothing else in this world matters. You are all I ever had. You are my son. I swore to Molly that I would never tell. But I have to. On the day you were born Canepole was happy. But not none so happy as me. I'm proud of you. You have a great heart. You are the best swimmer, the best fisherman, the best horseman, and almost the best storyteller. I love you. Please forgive me. Please come see your father. I'll be at our old hideout on the river.

Love Forever,

Moses

P. S.   I still have Duke's flask."

After Hook finished reading he lifted three saddlebags. From one of them he pulled out a silver flask, engraved, DUKE. "When I went to Buster's cabin near the Winding Staircase I found the three horses that he had brought back from the murder scene. Among some of

313

the personal belongings, I found the letter I just read--it was in the sheriff's saddlebags--I also found the flask in the deputy's--All three saddlebags had blood on them." Hook held up the flask for everyone to see. There, in its center going all the way through, a perfect bullet hole; he stuck his finger through it, showing the court. Hook continued. "I didn't figure things out until it was too late—after I had caught Ed, I left him with the posse and on my way coming back, I found the trail that the sheriff and his two deputies had taken going up to Proctor. They had met someone camped near the river. Their three horses had ridden in and when they rode out those same horses were packing more weight as their tracks were heavier. I followed the trail that they had taken to the river and I found an abandoned campsite of one man. At the water's edge I saw where the high weeds were bent over. I can't say for certain—I didn't find any blood--but it appeared like a body had been dragged through and dumped."

Ed was stunned as his family looked bewildered and his mother bawled.

"COME ON JUDGE!" hollered Irvine's new and first time barberer, Rusty McCallister, a bald headed scarecrow wearing thick glasses, positioned somewhere in the balcony. "I'VE BEEN STRUCK BY LIGHTNING SEVEN TIMES BUT I AINT NEVER BEEN STRUCK BY SO MUCH JABBER! WE'RE THIRSTY! WILL YOU PLEASE FINISH THIS THING!"

Quinn looked over at Joe Ohr. "That bunch of stuff you claim is really something, sure enough," he allowed. "But the fact still remains; Ed is a horse thief and a murderer. I now conclude that forty-five

314

days from today, May 29, 1857, noon, by the powers invested in me, forthwith and so forth, I sentence Ed to be hung by the neck until he is dead, may God have mercy on his soul."

Chapter Ninety Six

Taking Measure

Along about the second week that Ed was in his log cell the guard opened the door. "There are three men out here to measure you," he said, smiling. "I'm gonna let 'em in one at a time—they've all been searched--don't try nothing funny."

"Measure?" asked Ed.

"Yep, there's a coffin maker here to measure and make sure he doesn't waste any wood on you. There's the hangman that's got to measure and make sure he doesn't snap off your head. And there's an old preacher out here that's saying your soul needs to be measured."

"Tell them to go away," spoke Ed, despondent.

"ROTTEN AGES LEFT FOR ME, TELL ME WHERE OH WHIS-KEY!" sang the coffin maker.

Ed couldn't believe what he was hearing. "Let him in," he said.

"Sssh!" whispered Kit, holding his finger up to his mouth after he got in, continuing his whisper while taking measurements "Now listen, don't say nothing, I've got two out there with me, we've got it all figured sweet. Just do what we tell you and you'll come out of this fine."

Ed hugged Kit; tears poured out of his eyes.

"I AIN'T GOT ALL DAY," spoke the hangman. "LET ME IN THERE! I'M SUFFERING FROM THE MOST ABSOLUTE WORST CASE OF OPUS NEFAS THAT THERE HAS EVER BEEN," he announced.

The guard unlocked the door and let the hangman in.

Ed was waiting; it was Duke, alright.

"I'm going to hang you," whispered Duke. "That much is true. But all the weight is going to be on a leather vest and not on your neck. I've got a special vest for you—it'll be hid smart under your new suit. Don't worry, it works--I'll make certain. I better get out of here. There's a man that's been dying to see you. OPEN THE DOOR!"

"God's all tuckered out, my son," preached Moses as he came in and Duke went out. "And because he is, brave men like me have to clean up his mistakes. If you'll confess, I'll make certain that you have a particular new suit of clothes to be hanged in. Amen."

"Say, the flask, the hole through it, what happened?"

"Best shot I ever made. Don't think just because Hook is honest that he couldn't be bought—but damn, he's expensive."

"Good money?"

"Some of Duke's finest."

Chapter Ninety Seven

One Last Wish

"Guard," hollered Ed a few days after his three visitors had left. I've written a letter that I want you to give to the Judge. Ask him to please grant me one last wish and send it to my mother. Will you do that for me?

"Alright, But don't ask me for nothing else."

Dear Mom,

I love you. I have been the luckiest man alive to have two fathers: A father that was my uncle and an uncle that was my father. I loved them both. Don't ever forget me. And remember the good times. God never made a mother more beautiful than you. I am now chained in a cold tomb until brought out to die. But do not worry. I will be brave to the end. Please bury me with no marker for I shamed the family.

Ed

Chapter Ninety Eight

A Certain Bird

Ed continued listening to the crowd outside his cell grow louder; ten thousand human ticks all wanting his blood; he was now standing up having finished with his reverie of all that had transpired over the past forty-five days. The guard said there were more than ten thousand gathered to watch. The hanging had developed into something of a drunken Mushroom Festival; everybody had combed the hills for them; most of the mushrooms that they were eating were the wrong kind--but the right kind for this day; every squalid soul from every sordid region was salivating to see death; the "liar's benches" in front of the courthouse had all collapsed.

When Ed stepped out of his cell in his new suit and his hair all slicked back a long silence fell.

Ed looked up, squinting at a pale sky; the first time in nearly two months his eyes had been free; it was such a fine day.

Many girls came up one at a time giving Ed kisses, a long line of gals, sobbing and bidding goodbyes.

Nobody was as brave as him.

He stood there, every inch, solid Kentucky.

He was the most handsome man in the state; a face that owned all the grace of the state, a balance of wild beginning in those eyelashes and the brightness in his eyes, a sunrise on the river. And black was his hair; a field of black weeds growing proud; his face was the cliffs that Canepole always dove off; cliffs alone to themselves, smooth, tall, volunteered from the woods, guarding the river; such a fine face of invite but lonely; no hollow darker or whippoorwill more sad... and sweet dimples turning a day around from nary bite to a bent pole…and lips plump, begging to love him tender.

Ed walked down some steps to an oxcart holding his coffin to which he was chained. Beside it was Kit that snuck him a wink. Ed stood on top of it looking out at all the faces. "COME SEE A BRAVE MAN FACE DEATH," he shouted; wildflowers commenced being laid down until they piled up to his knees.

Along a rough up and down dirt road, the cart slowly pressed on, bouncing in and out of ruts; the flowers were falling off and more being added on; the crowd continuing to move aside and follow for over two miles.

There was one man in attendance believing that he'd do some good with his son, showing him where sin leads. But that man became sorry he ever brought his boy as Ed was being hailed as some kind of hero; it was as though Kentucky herself was being hanged.

And another fellow messed up likewise; he brought in his daughters and wife and before he knew it they were all crying and wishing they could free Ed; one of them saying that she'd like to run off with him.

Ed wasn't about to let his family down; nothing about any Hawkins could ever be associated with a coward. "I"M NOT A-FEARED!" he

continued to yell out to the crowd. "I'M GOIN' HOME! EVERY-
THANG IS FINE!"

When Ed got to the gallows there it all was, thirteen steps leading
up to a rope with thirteen loops; standing on one side of the rope was
Duke and on the other side, Moses—only now Moses wasn't Moses;
he was disguised as some kind of Bishop wearing a strange, tall hat
that some of those religious higher-ups with strong necks sometimes
used. And he was now being known as, Bishop Callerhan. Off from
them down on the ground was Molly holding the reins to Jenny. "I'VE
NEVER SEEN A BRAVER MAN!" shouted Kit out to the crowd as
he held onto the coffin looking up at Ed.

A quarter of a mile away, Estill's new Sheriff, "Possum" Puckett,
was having a rough time with the Judge as his Honor was drowsy,
queer as if he had been drugged; so drowsy that it was impossible for
him to move, let alone attend the hanging.

Moses looked out into the packed crowd. "MY GREAT CHRIS-
TIAN FRIENDS," he eloquently thundered. "PLEASE LISTEN
TO WHAT I MUST SAY BEFORE THIS POOR YOUNG MAN
PASSES ON INTO THAT DEEP ABYSS OF ETERNIY. AS
YOU ALL KNOW, OLD MEN HAVE POOR VISION. THE
OLDER THEY GET THE WORSE THEIR VISION BECOMES.
AMEN. AND AS YOU ALL CAN AGREE, GOD IS THE OLD-
EST MAN THERE IS. AND BECAUSE HE IS SO ANCIENT
AND HIS EYES SO BAD IT IS HIGH TIME THAT HE RE-
CEIVES A PAIR OF GLASSES. NOT JUST ANY GLASSES BUT
THE VERY FINEST THAT MONEY CAN BUY. HE NEEDS A

323

STRONG PAIR SO THAT HE CAN SEE JUST WHAT A BAD MESS THIS WORLS HAS BECOME. AFTER HIS EYES GETS THOSE GLASSES THEN HE'LL COME DOWN HERE AND FIX THINGS. I AM NOW ASKING THAT ANY OF YOU WITH CASH TO STEP FORWARD AND PUT YOUR MONEY IN ED'S OPEN COFFIN. DIG DEEP INTO YOUR POCKETS AND GIVE ALL THAT YOU HAVE. NOT JUST TO GET GOD THOSE GLASSES HE SO BADLY NEEDS BUT ALSO TO AS-SURE YOURSELF A FRONT ROW SEAT IN HEAVEN. GOD WILL REMEMBER THOSE THAT HELPED HIM. AND WHEN YOU GET UP THERE AND STAND BEFORE SAINT PETER GOD WILL TELL HIM WHAT YOU DID AND WILL OR-DER HIM TO OPEN UP THOSE PEARLY GATES. SO, DEAR FRIENDS, STEP FORTH, FILL THAT COFFIN UP. ALLOW GOD TO KNOW WHO IS ON HIS SIDE IN THIS WORLD THAT CAN ONLY BE DESCRIBED AS NEFARIOUS. AMEN."

"Any last words?" asked Duke as he carefully placed the rope down over Ed's head.

Ed looked out at so many faces and then up into the sky. Up there, ever so high, he could see a certain bird…

Chesteen and No Sweat.

Author of THESE PRECIOUS DAYS, NEFARIOUS, BLACK
BLUEGRASS,   UNBRIDLED, LETTERS FROM A GENIUS TO
AN OAF, PIGEON and ES#1 THE PRYSE SITE.

Interests: WRITING, ARCHEOLOGY, RACING PIGEONS,
SCUBA DIVING, CIVIL WAR, KENTUCKY RED AGATE, LOB-
STERS, SPELUNKING,INDIAN RELICS, FOSSILS, BOATING,
OLD MOVIES.PHOTOGRAPHY, SWIMMING, HORSE RACING,
REVOLUTIONARY WAR, METAL DETECTING, SOUTHERN
FLORIDA, BIRDS

CPSIA information can be obtained at www.ICGtesting.com
Printed in the USA
LVOW050037010513

331535LV00002B/69/P